NIGHTHUNTER 5
The Hexing

Also in Arrow by Robert Faulcon

NIGHTHUNTER 5

The Hexing

Robert Faulcon

ARROW BOOKS

Arrow Books Limited
17–21 Conway Street, London W1P 6JD

An imprint of the Hutchinson Publishing Group

London Melbourne Sydney Auckland
Johannesburg and agencies throughout
the world

First published 1984

© Robert Faulcon 1984

Set in Plantin by Photobooks (Bristol) Ltd

Printed and bound in Great Britain by
Anchor Brendon Limited, Tiptree, Essex

ISBN 0 09 939960 1

For Anne of the Thousand Runes

PROLOGUE
The Nightmare

The nightmare always begins with a vision of the garden of his house, Brook's Corner. It is a few days before Christmas. The garden is covered with a fine layer of snow, and his young daughter Marianna, in her bulky overcoat and scarf, is pelting him with snowballs. She giggles and runs as he pursues her, jumping onto the coal bunker, and then onto the shed, out of his reach. Her eyes sparkle with mischief behind her small round-framed spectacles. In the nightmare he can still feel the snow trickling down his neck where her last snowball caught him good and true.

There is a flash of light in the grey afternoon. Alison has photographed them, the first Christmas memory. It's too cold to stay out in the grounds and they go inside, to sit around the blazing log fire.

This is always the first thing that he sees in the dream, the echo of that last moment of happiness. Then there is the image of the Christmas tree and its decorations, of young Dominick by the fire, cutting up last year's greeting cards, of Alison peeling chestnuts and humming to herself. Outside, just evening darkness.

'Where's Marianna?'

No one speaks. And in that moment of silence, the fire flickering, the room warm, there is a strong sense of impending disaster.

Dominick's voice is cold and distant. 'There was a man outside . . . she was talking to him.'

His gaze meets Alison's. In that instant they know, they both know.

In the dream her face is never the same – sometimes terrified, sometimes blank, sometimes sad.

He comes down the ladder. His son seems embarrassed. The room swims around him and Alison's terror-stricken face looms large.

'My daughter . . .' she says. 'Oh my God . . .'

Then, in the nightmare, there is the memory of Marianna calling them. She is standing outside the french windows, crying behind her tiny, round-framed glasses. She looks very small, very pretty, very vulnerable.

'Daddy! I'm cold!'

'MARIANNA!' he screams, and there is an explosion of glass, then darkness. He can never forget the way his tiny daughter was flung against him by an invisible power. He can't forget the way she was carried by a dark-robed shape, out into the cold night. As hands try to strangle him he watches the abduction of his wife and son as well, both of them knocked senseless and dragged away by men who have the faces of animals.

Then there is fire. The edges of the nightmare begin to burn furiously. Through the flames he sees the pattern of an ancient labyrinth, painted onto the killers' dark robes. He hears the name *Magondathog*, a place of ultimately awesome power. He hears a woman's voice. He hears his own mind screaming with confusion.

Who are they? Why us? How dare they do this to us?

This is how the nightmare ends, with a primal scream of anger and terror.

Yes. That's right, that's quite right. Good. But what else? What has been added to the nightmare? Can you tell me that?

Some of the questions have been answered. The dark force is called Arachne, and its coming has been known for centuries.

Yes . . .

Their purpose is to resurrect a total magic, using the forces, demons and secret knowledge of all the different cultures of history. Total magic. Total eclipse. Their purpose is an Awakening. Their purpose is to control the World Mind . . .

Yes. At least, that's what he believes . . .

His daughter has a special talent, useful to them. His

8

family has been scattered. Dominick is on an island in the west. The girl is in the north. Alison . . . is in London. This much he knows. But time is running out. Something called the *Roundelay* is coming closer. A time of change. He will lose them, then. He will lose them totally, and he knows it.

Good. Very good. I think you'll do.

There is something I don't understand. They took his family, but not Dan Brady himself. Why?

Because they are too confident. Because they are not yet organised completely. Arachne meant to kill Brady, and they failed. They still make mistakes.

So Brady has no role to play.

He has the most important role of all. He is the Hunter, now. The Night Hunter. He is Arachne's own growing nightmare.

He is their nemesis.

PART ONE
The Hexing

1

Four days after Judge 'Tip' McGeary's death, the four remaining members of his Special Action Squad, known as Death Unit 2000, met at their new headquarters, a small room above 38 Chelsea Avenue. Gerry Cronin, appointed Judge only two weeks before, made the necessary contacts and arrangements. The emergency session was scheduled for 10 a.m. on Saturday.

As he waited for Troopers Hughes and Thompson, and the new Prospect (or rookie), Thompson's sister, Judge Cronin prepared the room for what he imagined would be a tense and angry debate about future tactics. He erected a blackboard and wrote out, in red chalk, the four governing principles – the Code – by which the group operated. He placed pencils and paper around the edge of the small conference table, and piled canned drinks in the middle.

He turned an Angle-Poise lamp onto the huge poster-portrait of their mentor, a tall, angry man dressed in the dark leather and yellow limb-protectors of a Judge.

Then, after saluting the picture of Dredd, Judge Cronin buckled on his gun-belt, with its heavy, holstered weapon. He slipped his helmet over his head, pulling down the tinted visor.

Cronin was a tall, broad-shouldered man with an easy, lithe gait. His fair hair was tightly curled about his head, and his eyes were pale blue, giving them a piercing quality that was at once fearsome and remote. With McGeary dead he was the new leader of the Squad. But a power struggle had been on the cards, anyway. The two Judges had begun to contest control of Death Unit 2000, and a bitter duel would have been organised in a few weeks.

Now, though, the hatred between the two men was forgotten. McGeary was dead and Cronin would avenge that death. He would pursue no further ambitions until the ghost of Tip McGeary was laid quietly to rest.

Behind him, the window was rapped. He turned, eyes narrowing, hand drifting to the heavy stock of his high-calibre Magnum. The coded signal was tapped out: three short, two long, three short.

Cronin walked briskly to the shutters of the window and opened them. Trooper Hughes was balanced precariously on the ladder, trying to salute. Cronin opened the window and the Squad's hit man crawled in to safety.

Ritchie Hughes was a pale-skinned and stocky man. He had a pugnacious face, and eyes that were shifty and narrow. The hand that clasped Cronin's was twice the size of the taller man's, pudgy and clammy. Hughes was breathing heavily and a sheen of sweat had formed below his short, dark hair.

Judge Cronin didn't particularly trust the trooper, but he liked him. Hughes was strong. He was used as the Squad's muscle, and was effective and well feared. He was also good at acquiring equipment for Death Unit 2000's raids.

'Trooper Hughes reporting for duty!' Hughes said by way of greeting, looking hungrily around the small room. Then he saw the huge picture of Judge Dredd and his eyes widened with astonished delight. 'Where did you get *that?*' he said in slow admiration.

Cronin swaggered behind the fat man. 'Booty,' he said. 'A raid last Tuesday.'

Hughes glanced round, away from the proud figure of the man who was their hero. He looked slightly frightened.

'Day of Tip's death.'

'Yes,' Cronin said grimly.

Trooper Hughes stared up at the portrait again, sniffing loudly. He used a finger and thumb to squeeze his nostrils, then wiped his hand on his jeans.

'It's Tip's birthday next Wednesday.'

'I know,' Cronin said softly. He clasped his hands

14

behind his back, military style. The memory of good times was painful. Hughes was feeling McGeary's death acutely. He missed Tip a lot.

'He'd have been ten,' Ritchie Hughes said, almost despairingly. 'He'd have been an adult!'

'A good man,' Gerry Cronin said. His own tenth birthday was still five months away. 'I hope my leadership will be as worthy.'

Ritchie turned dark, angry eyes on him. '*Your* leadership?'

'Mine,' Gerry Cronin said coolly, favouring the fat boy with his coldest stare. 'I'm a Judge, remember? I take over from now.'

'This was Tip's gang!' Ritchie said indignantly, squeezing his nose again and wiping his hand on his trousers. But before he could say more, before the tension could develop into physical hostility, the secret code was rapped out on the window and Gerry went over to admit the last two members of Death Unit 2000.

First through the window was the Prospect. Her name was Philippa Victoria Thompson. She was eight, pushing nine years old, and taller by an inch or so than Ritchie Hughes. Her nickname was Pippa. Her hair was tightly ringleted, the ringlets forming cords across her scalp – a typical and traditional West Indian hair-style. Her eyes and mouth were wide; she had an adult look, and an interested one.

The first thing she did as she stood in Gerry's room was giggle, a sound she stifled. It was Gerry in his comic-book uniform that had set her off and the boy stiffened with irritation, the more so since Ritchie was sharing her humour.

Unbuttoning her orange anorak, the girl waited expectantly for things to happen. It was her first meeting with the boys, although she had come on two raids with them in the last two weeks. The boy who had died, Tip, had been very good to her, very kind.

Behind her, her brother, Errol 'Flynn' Thompson, sprang into the room, straightening up and saluting.

15

Gerry and Ritchie saluted back, then exchanged the Death Unit 2000 handshake with him.

Flynn looked around and gasped with more childlike astonishment than any of the others. He had never seen inside the Cronins' house and was totally unaware of the extent to which Gerry's room was a shrine to the comic that they adored, *2000 AD*, whose characters – from Judge Dredd to the RoboHunters – had inspired their squad structure and informed the imaginative beliefs of their games. Flynn was really Ritchie Hughes' friend. They were in the same class at school and had known each other for a year or more. Gerry Cronin was cool towards him. It was partly that he had less in common with Flynn than either of them had with the pudgy Hughes boy, and partly that his parents had actively discouraged him from playing with the black family from a few streets away.

As much as Gerry Cronin was aware of social politics at the age of nine and a half, he was aware that his father was hideously prejudiced.

Flynn prowled around the room, his breath a series of excited wheezes. He wore a simple leather blouson over a white tee-shirt, and short, faded denims. Gerry stared at him, aware, somehow, that Flynn was what was referred to at school as 'sharp'. He suddenly felt a little ludicrous in the outfit he had painstakingly copied from the comic.

'You got some good things!' Flynn enthused, and when he looked at the white boy his eyes were glowing with a naive pleasure that made up for a lot of Gerry's growing jealousy. 'Look at these *comics*! Hoe. Lee. *Shit*!' Flynn picked up a handful from the four shelves of *2000 AD*, *The Shadow*, *Warrior* and *Weird Tales*. His voice, that of a child in tone, was a vivid echo of the older boys from the local school.

Pippa just sat and stared at the poster of Judge Dredd. Suddenly she started to cry. Ritchie Hughes put his arm around her shoulder.

'We'll find out what happened to Tip,' he said, trying to be reassuring. Pippa just shrugged, sniffed, then shook off the boy's embrace.

'Let's get down to the meeting,' Gerry said. Ritchie and Pippa sat at the table. Flynn replaced the comics and took one more slow circuit round the room, staring at the posters of the Mighty Tharg, the Strontium Dogs, Johnny Alpha and Wulf, the autographed portraits of Walter the Robot and Ro-Jaws. Finally he keyed a simple instruction on Gerry's Commodore 64 micro-computer.

'You even got a Commodore! All I got's a Sinclair. No VDU, no fun. But you got one. Can I use it sometime?' He glanced at Gerry, who shrugged.

'OK. First, though, we have a mission.'

'Yeah. Tip.'

Flynn sat down, picked up a pencil and began to sketch a pistol on the paper before him. Gerry took off his helmet and placed it on the table.

'Trooper Flynn, will you keep a recording of this emergency session?'

'OK,' said Flynn. Gerry placed a compact cassette recorder on the table and set it going. Flynn placed a finger on the pause switch, ready to stop the recording of anything that might have given the enemy a vital clue as to their raiding plans for the future. Gerry turned the poster of Judge Dredd round and exposed their secret map of North London.

'Somebody killed our colleague and friend, Aiden Tip McGeary,' Gerry said carefully, and Pippa began to cry again, her lips trembling, tears rolling from her eyes. Her brother glared at her, nudging her hard, and she sniffed loudly, glancing at him resentfully, but stopped the flow of tears.

Gerry stood in front of the map and looked at his attentive squad. 'We've got to find out how and why Tip died.'

'Somebody followed him from the Wasteland,' Ritchie said. 'Somebody's hiding there and Tip – I mean, Judge McGeary – disturbed them. A Mutant, probably. Or a crazed Robot.'

'I ain't going nowhere where there's no things like *that*!' Pippa said, looking anxiously at her brother.

'Troopers go where they're sent,' Flynn said, slightly embarrassed by his sister's outburst.

The girl pouted, shrinking into herself as she watched Gerry Cronin. 'I ain't getting involved with Mutants,' she murmured. 'Or Robots. Or Strontium Dogs. No way.'

'We've all got to find out what killed Tip,' Ritchie said. 'Anyway, Prospects always stay on look-out duty.'

Gerry tapped a wooden pointer on the map. 'Stop talking in the ranks,' he said, trying to inject severity into his childish voice, 'and concentrate on this. What do we know about what happened to Tip? Trooper Flynn?'

Flynn stood up, hands by his side. 'He was running away from the Mutie Wasteland. He was very frightened when I saw him last.'

'Did he say what'd scared him?'

'He said . . .' Flynn frowned and thought hard for a moment. 'He said he'd found a river. That's it. A river. He said he'd been searching for Mutants and found a hidden doorway, and there was a river beyond it.'

Gerry waited but Flynn had said his piece. 'Trooper Hughes? You saw Tip on the same day.'

Ritchie stood up. His face was damp and his big hands bunched up into fists. 'Yes sir,' he said. 'He was very scared. He was at home, hiding in his room. He said there'd been an old lady and a dog, who'd chased him. He said they were going to kill him. I had to go and get some takeaway stuff from Macdonald's and the next thing I knew . . .' He looked down, shaking slightly. 'My mum told me.'

'That's how I heard,' Gerry said, suddenly ashen-faced. 'Torn open, like by a wild animal. But I heard my dad talking and he said he'd been strangled first.'

Pippa whimpered slightly, but stopped when her brother elbowed her.

Gerry pointed to the map, to the narrow stretch of overgrown and unused old railway track that curled through the area of North London, close to where they lived. This haven for exploration and hiding was practically invisible from anywhere but the air. When Tip

18

discovered it, a year or more ago, it had been deserted, and there were no signs of any other kids having been there. It was their private wasteland, a place that they had made as secret as their organisation. They *did* occasionally see people moving about in the tangle of bush and tree that filled the cutting, but that all added to the game: raids into the Mutie Wasteland, the indefatigable Judges and their escort of Troopers, making sure that the brutal and brutalised remnants of the Third World War didn't enter the streets of the civilised.

Over the year, in the evenings and at weekends, they had thoroughly explored the square mile or so of London that spread out around the steep rise of the hill where they lived. Some streets were posh, with large houses almost hidden by trees. Others were rows of virtual slums. Richness and poverty ran, it seemed, at right angles to each other, and this was reflected in the members of Death Unit 2000. The Thompsons and the Hughes lived in ramshackle terraced houses, with tiny back-gardens overlooking the red-brick walls of small industry. Four hundred yards away from the Thompsons, the Cronin family lived in semi-detached splendour; their garden had a barbecue pit and a pond. They owned two cars.

In the same affluent street which the Cronins inhabited there was a 'safe' house for the members of the squad, a deserted house with a loose cellar cover. The children used it occasionally, but it was a risky place because every few days an old man came and checked that everything was secure inside. They had nearly been caught on two occasions.

They had several other very safe, and very secret, hide-outs, from the unused garden patch behind a row of garages to the deserted, dark and surprisingly cosy basement rooms of a house conversion. There was also the underground room-complex of an abandoned industrial site. Here, Death Unit 2000 had stored food and other supplies ready for a long siege.

All of these places had codenames: Trog City, Airbase 50, Fort Alpha and so on. Gerry now ran through the

Unit's strategy for using these safe patches, pointing to each on the map as he swaggered about in front of the group. In the event that they, too, should find themselves pursued and forced to scatter, they would meet first at Airbase 50, or if that failed, at Fort Alpha.

Unless things got exceptionally dangerous, Trog City would *not* be used.

The plan of action, then, would be to enter the Wasteland by the Tunnel Zone (a steep embankment leading down to the rails of the London Underground system, then a brief walk through the darkness of a tunnel to the access passage leading into the overgrown cutting) and work steadily through it, looking for a river . . . and for Tip's killer.

Gerry Cronin quickly changed his clothes for garments more suitable to the cold weather outside. Then he led the way from the Unit's HQ, down the ladder to the garden, and round the side passage to the street. They walked quickly away from the house and when they were out of eye-shot they broke into a run.

The route to the Wasteland took them past Tip's house, and they all slowed down and stared morosely at the small garden, with its rose bushes and dwarf ferns. The curtains of the house were still closed, but as they watched so the front door opened and Tip's father came out, dressed in an overcoat and carrying a shopping bag. He wore dark glasses.

'Hello, kids,' he said softly as he walked past them to the shops.

'Hello, Mr McGeary,' they all said back. For a moment the man and the children hesitated, looking at each other as if there might be something more to say. Then the man said, 'Don't go too far. The police haven't found who did it yet.'

'No, sir,' Gerry said.

Pippa said, 'We miss Tip.'

Mr McGeary smiled in a wan and sad way. 'Thank you,' he said, his voice a mere whisper. Then he turned and walked along the avenue.

Death Unit 2000 walked respectfully for a few yards past the house, then broke into a run.

The way down to the tracks was behind a large, weather-battered advertising hoarding. Behind the wooden façade was a high brick wall. By using the wooden struts in the advertising board, the wall could be scaled. On top there was a jagged layer of bottle glass. That negotiated, there was an eight-foot drop to the embankment, but Tip, after he'd discovered this route, had brought an old, rusting step-ladder from his parents' garage and hidden it in the brambles that swarmed across the slopes.

Gerry led the way to the rail tracks, dropping from the wall and searching quickly for any signs of railway personnel. He helped Pippa down, then Ritchie, then Flynn. A Northern Line train rattled past below them and they crouched, out of sight, behind a gorse-bush. Then they slid and scampered to the tracks, checked the tunnel for oncoming trains, and darted into the darkness.

Flynn almost had to drag his sister by the hand. She uttered no word of protest but was clearly reluctant to enter the Stygian gloom. Visions of Mutants and rampaging Robots were clear in her head. And thoughts of Tip, his face all black, his chest ripped open, made her whimper with apprehension.

'Come *on*!' her brother said. 'If you want to be a Trooper you mustn't show fear.'

'To feel fear is part of survival,' hissed Ritchie, quoting from a favourite John Wayne movie. 'It's OK, Pippa. We'll be OK.'

Gerry hushed them into silence. He had found the low arch that led away from the tube tunnel, and they felt their way steadily through it. Soon, light appeared ahead, and they emerged, triumphant, into the Wasteland.

For a minute or so they stood in semi-concealment and scanned the deep, narrow valley. Everything was silent; everything was motionless. Gerry indicated that Ritchie Hughes should cross the ground to the far side, and the stocky boy bent low and worked his way through the undergrowth until he fetched up against the sloping wall opposite.

In the distance, the cutting was crossed by a road bridge, which was protected from the drop by high metal walls. When a double-decker bus passed over the bridge, only the top of the deck could be seen, a slash of red passing quickly across the sky. The deserted track was lined on both sides by dark brick walls, which sloped steeply up for fifteen feet, before rising vertically for another twenty. Dark arches cut into the walls suggested passages, but they were all bricked off just inside.

Where the rail tracks had once been there was just a tangle of briar, whitethorn and self-seeded alder and lime trees, none of which had grown more than fifteen feet high. Tyres, rusting prams, tin cans, this was the sort of junk that the jungle was growing over, and most of it was very old. There was a ramshackle wooden hut a hundred yards down the valley. One of its windows still had glass in it, and inside there were musty, damp newspapers over ten years old, and a blackened milk-pan.

This was the squad's Wasteland rendezvous, and they gathered there now, glad to have made it this far from the Tunnel Zone.

They listened hard for a river, but could only hear traffic.

'If he was exploring, he probably went further down into the marshes,' Ritchie suggested. The marsh was an area of the railway cutting which was water-logged and unpleasant; it might also have been dangerous, since some of the stagnant pools were very deep.

'Let's go,' Gerry said, but Pippa tugged back.

'I ain't going no further,' she announced defiantly. Her pretty face was racked with apprehension. 'And don't you go either, Flynn.'

Her brother scowled, tugging his collar up around his neck and glancing irritably at Gerry. 'I'm going,' he said to his sister.

'You're an idiot,' she said huffily.

'I've got to help find out what Tip knew. You stay here, then, and keep watch. Whistle if you see anyone approaching.'

'You know I can't whistle.'

'Then shout,' Flynn said vehemently. The girl sat looking sullen, then turned away from him.

'If things get too scary,' Ritchie whispered to her, 'Then just shout to us, and then get back the way we came.'

'Nothing would *stop* me,' she said petulantly, folding her arms and drawing her legs up into a huddle as she sat by the hut's door.

Gerry and Flynn scampered off into the undergrowth. Ritchie followed, then turned and looked back at the girl, smiling. 'There aren't really any Mutants here,' he whispered.

'Something killed Tip,' she murmured after his darting shape. 'And it's gonna kill you too.'

It was Flynn who found it; and in a way, that wasn't surprising.

Three weeks ago, on one of their staged raids beyond the marshes, Flynn had noticed Judge McGeary tugging and heaving at something which was hidden behind a thicket of bramble at the side of the steep wall. He had heard Tip's gasp of disgust and smelled a little of the foul odour that the other boy had released by shifting some weight, or door, and exposing what lay below.

Before they could investigate further, Ritchie, on lookout duty, had seen movement in the distance, away from the Tunnel Zone, and they had beaten a fast retreat.

They had been tired, they'd had a lot of fun; the smell, and whatever Tip had discovered, remained unmentioned, and more or less forgotten by Flynn.

Now he found his way to the same spot and began to poke around in the thorny undergrowth, wary of broken bottles or spikes of metal. Soon he found what he was looking for.

He kicked back the briar, and stamped down the nettles

that grew abundantly there. Behind them was an area where the dark-bricked wall had been roughly cut out and a heavy wooden door installed. Everything was filthy, and the hinges on the door were almost black with rust. Flynn got an impression that the work had been done years and years ago. But his attention was taken more immediately by the funny markings on the door. They looked as if they had been carved with a knife, and they sent shivers up and down his spine . . .

They looked like hex marks, like the witch marks that he'd seen in the books that his parents kept in their bedroom: a series of crosses in crude circles, reversed letters, and a spidery pattern that looked like the maze game where you had to follow one line right through. Below them all was a roughly drawn image that made Flynn's blood turn to ice: three joined skulls, one staring at him, the other two looking to the sides. They were not human skulls; they were the skulls of dogs.

As he reached to touch the doorway he noticed that his hand was shaking violently. He felt extremely cold, colder than the autumn day should have been able to manage. In fact, his breath had started to frost in front of his face and he backed off from the hex-marked wood with something like an alarmed cry.

Ritchie Hughes stopped beating through the briar tangles on the other side of the cutting and began to walk over to him.

'What've you got, Flynn?'

'Nothing . . .' Flynn said quickly, but by now Gerry Cronin had caught the sense of concern emerging from the West Indian boy, and was trotting back to him, body stooped, stick held in both hands like a soldier running with a rifle.

'What is it?'

Ritchie shrugged, staring at Flynn. 'Flynn cried out.' His gaze flickered beyond the nervous boy, and a moment later he saw the door, almost totally hidden again behind the tangled growth of thorny scrub.

'Hey! Look at that!'

'Leave it alone,' Flynn said nervously. 'It's got hex marks on it.'

From a distance they heard Pippa calling. They couldn't make out her words, but she sounded angry and fed up. Flynn guessed she was announcing her return to the main road. He felt better about that. He wanted her out of this overgrown wilderness as soon as possible.

He wanted himself out of here too. He could hardly bring himself to look at the triple-skull image, but each time he glanced at it the jaws seemed to open and snap at him, making him shudder with an awful apprehension.

But Ritchie Hughes was now tugging at the door, and with Gerry's help they dislodged it from its setting. It creaked furiously and moved just an inch or so. Both boys gagged, then laughed and staggered back for a moment, holding hands to their faces. Flynn caught the aroma and recognised it. The closest smell he could identify with it was the smell of putrefaction, most commonly associated, in his street, with a dead cat left to rot at the roadside because no one would touch it.

This smell was worse. Something told him that there was a dead man inside the passageway.

Ritchie had edged back to the door. 'These are weird,' he said, running two stubby fingers over the crude knife-carvings.

'It's a Mutie stronghold,' Gerry said, but Ritchie shrugged the comment off. The marks were for real. This was no part of their Death Unit 2000 fantasy.

'I can hear water,' Ritchie said. He made a disgusted expression. 'That *smell*!' His face wrinkled up. His hand over his nose, he jerked the door open a little wider. Gerry crouched behind him, peering into the gloom.

'That's the river! Tip said he'd heard a river . . .'

'Or a sewer,' Ritchie said. Flynn approached cautiously behind them, glancing anxiously around, almost convinced that they would be surprised by a railway official, or a tramp . . . or whoever had strangled Tip McGeary. 'Don't go inside,' he whispered, but Gerry just waved him into silence.

25

Now they did what Tip had failed to do. They wrenched the door open wide enough for a man to step inside. The sound of rushing, bubbling water was louder, but it was coming from a long way off. Flynn also thought he could hear a dull padding sound. As Ritchie entered the maw of the dark place, Flynn found himself desperately torn between allegiance: he was part of the Squad and should not show fear; but he was also an intelligent boy who trusted his instincts, and his instinct at that moment was to run.

Gerry Cronin hissed at him, 'Flynn. Trooper Flynn! Come on.'

Flynn edged forward, following his two friends, who had already stepped into the passageway beyond the hex-marked door. The smell had faded slightly, but it still made him gag. The sound of the river was magnified as he came into the cavern. He could hear Ritchie and Gerry shuffling through the darkness ahead.

'It's like a tunnel,' Gerry whispered. 'It leads down to the water. I can see it. There.'

Flynn, close to the entrance and still glancing anxiously behind him, had not let his eyes adjust sufficiently to see the distant vague glimmer of the running water, deep below the hill. 'Let's get out of here,' he hissed urgently, dropping to a crouch and leaning on the ground. The other boys ignored him until he gave a sudden yelp of shock.

He had touched something on the ground, looked down, and seen what it was. A human skull, a thin layer of parchment-dry skin and wispy hair still attached to the bone!

'Shit!' he yelled, and stood, knocking his head on the low rock roof. 'Oh *shit*!'

Pain, and a mind-sound like thunder, made him stagger about the confined space. He kicked something, and from the corner of his eye saw a small white shape roll away, a dog's head, severed, drawn and hideous.

The thunder came again, making him screech with shock. He was aware of Ritchie Hughes' face looming out of the darkness at him. The boy was terror-stricken, eyes bulging, mouth open and slickly wet. Behind him there was a sudden eerie silver light. It was flooding up the sloping tunnel, like a car streaking towards them. He could hear the heavy footfall of animals, and a deep baying sound, like the cry of an Alsatian dog, but somehow much more terrifying.

'It's an old hag!' Ritchie gasped, and pushed past Flynn to the daylight. Flynn followed without hesitation, without care, bruising himself twice more on jagged edges of rock.

Once outside, both boys stopped. Ritchie was shaking violently. Flynn noticed the bruises on his shoulder and head for the first time and rubbed them vigorously.

'What d'you mean? An old hag . . .'

Ritchie was incoherent as he spoke, his whole body drenched with sweat. Then his eyes widened in horror, looking past Flynn to the concealed passage. He turned and ran, then, and Flynn ran too, but not before he had seen the strange silver glow spilling from the area of brick and bush that surrounded the door.

A moment later, Gerry Cronin ran frantically into the daylight. He screamed to the others to wait, but Flynn and Ritchie Hughes were by now yards away, speeding to what they hoped would be safety.

Flynn stopped just once to catch his breath. When he looked back he saw the shining figure of a woman drifting towards them. Four immense black hounds, their jaws and tongues lolling, were leaping through the undergrowth that filled the Wasteland in a bizarre movement reminiscent of slow motion in a film. Gerry, blood all over his face, was running hysterically ahead of them.

Flynn saw the woman's face and nearly gagged. Old was not the word! She looked like a living corpse, her livid skin crawling with worm-life, her eyes the deep dull of death, yet aware of what they saw. Her smile was a death's head rictus, with yellow teeth gleaming.

Around her was the eerie moonglow, an aura of shimmering silver.

Flynn turned tail and ran on. A few yards behind

Ritchie he reached the Tunnel Zone. The fat boy was already scrabbling his way through the darkness. Behind Flynn, Gerry Cronin's yelling changed to a hysterical scream, and then a strangled wail. Glancing back, the West Indian boy was almost sick to see his friend's body *burning*. Gerry's arms were raised above his head. Silvery flame flickered over the body, his skin blackening and blistering, then turning to a reflective silvery white. His head and hands dropped limply.

Before his body could slump, one of the mastiffs leapt onto him and closed its jaws around his throat, worrying and shaking at the body. The other dogs kept on.

Flynn didn't wait about.

He passed through the Tunnel Zone, conscious of nothing but the demonic howling of the beasts which pursued him. He scrambled up the embankment, where Ritchie was already climbing over the glass-topped wall. Pippa, crouched on the same wall, was yelling fiercely. By the time Flynn had reached her she was sobbing violently. Then she stopped, her whole face registering horrified shock.

Flynn glanced down the embankment.

One of the dogs stood there, sniffing the air, growling deep in its throat as it watched the children above it.

A moment later it turned and vanished back into the tunnel.

2

Someone was shaking him. The grip on his shoulder was strong, the action vigorous. A voice urged, 'Dan! Wake up, Dan!'

As he surfaced from dream-state to reality so his nervous system jumped. For an instant he found himself standing by the bed, staring at his own sleeping body, and at the young woman who crouched over him, her hand on his naked shoulder. She was small, dark-haired, wearing jeans and a bulky jumper.

Then the eyes in his body opened and the extra-corporeal observer was snatched back into the grey matter of the waking man.

Brady jumped more physically and twisted round where he lay cocooned in wool blankets. He blinked at Anita Herbert, who smiled and kissed him quickly on the forehead.

'At *last*! Come on, Dan. You're going to be late.'

'What time – ? Oh Jesus!'

'Right,' Anita said severely. 'Nine fifteen. You've got forty-five minutes to make the appointment.'

Brady sat up, scratching his face and then rubbing his eyes. His whole body felt tired, his joints aching, his head filled with clouds. 'Shit!' he said. 'Why didn't you wake me before?'

Anita gasped incredulously, punching him on the chest as he began to untangle the blankets from around his torso. 'I've been trying for an hour!' she protested. 'You were in one of those deep whatsits . . . trance-sleeps. You should cut down on the psychic stuff.'

Brady couldn't help smiling at her expression: psychic stuff. Cut down on the psychic stuff, like some people ought to cut down on their intake of carbohydrates. There was no doubt that he was indulging too much in his new preoccupation of trying to increase and extend his own limited psychic power. It was having a bad effect upon him: weariness, premature ageing (he was now quite silver at the temples; a year ago, before the tragedy, his hair had been gleaming black) and the tendency to sleep in a deeper state than was normal.

There was another side-effect as well. The image was strong in his mind of that fleeting instant, a minute ago, when he had slipped from his body and watched himself waking up. The sensation was very strange. He normally had consciously to control the experience, but increasingly it was happening without him being aware of it. It was a powerful survival technique in some circumstances – in others, it could well be a burden. His physical corpse was stationary and vulnerable during the out-of-body float. That might not always be the safest defence against an attacker!

'Do I always sleep with my mouth open?' he asked the girl. Anita laughed.

'Why do you ask?'

'Well. It looks . . . ugly.'

She nodded soberly, her eyes twinkling. 'It's not ugly. It's just funny. Sometimes I try and see how many peanuts I can get in before you blow them out . . .'

'Liar!' He flung a pillow at the girl, who deftly avoided it. A year ago he would have chased her, caught her, and tumbled her, laughing, to the bed. But a year ago Anita Herbert would not have been in his life. He had been a family man, contented with home and with his work for the Ministry of Defence's paranormal research station at Hillingvale.

That contentment had ended in an abrupt, disgusting and devastating way last Christmas. His own life had hung in the balance for three months. When he had recovered from the attack upon him he had returned to an empty and silent world, alone and with only the blackest of memories.

Those images of the violent assault and abduction of his

30

family were always present in his mind's eye, and they stopped him, now, from enjoying the moment of levity with the girl.

Brady stood up from the bed and stretched. He was a tall and lean man, very agile and strong. The marks of the psychic attack upon him were still evident, in the fierce red weals around his wrists and neck. His eyes were bright but cold, deep set in a face that was dark-lined and drawn, all signs of the fear that haunted him, and the anger he still felt.

He tugged on his clothes without washing. Anita made him a mug of coffee and two pieces of cheese on toast. Clutching this simple breakfast he followed the girl down the stairs and into the lounge. She had opened the french windows and the room was airing. It was a cool day outside, dull and overcast. In the lounge was the merest hint of some herb being burnt, and Brady smiled.

Anita had been doing her chores.

He stepped outside and breathed in deeply, liking the cold assault of the air in his lungs. He would just have to be late for his appointment with the young medium, Stefan Taber. The man refused to have a phone and the arrangements had been made by letter. Right now, checking the psychic defences around the house and grounds was more important. It was a task that could never be neglected.

Anita watched him, a petulant frown on her face.

'If you're going to double-check everything I do,' she said, 'then do it yourself in the first place!'

Brady was peering into a glass-covered container. Inside, spread thinly on the base of the box, was a layer of iron filings mixed with finely pounded mandrake ash. In the event of any probe or tentative visitation by an actively psychic person, or the mental projection of psychic power, the layer would be thrown up into wave-like ripples. It wasn't a defence, it was a signalling device.

'I'd double-check even myself,' he said, straightening up. 'If it makes you feel any better, I'd *triple*-check anyone else! Come with me.'

Anita followed him into the garden, stepping carefully across the inner layer of defences, a maze-like pattern delicately cut into the turf and ground that touched the house itself. The *mazon*. Across this zone, Anita had already laid out the strands of copper wire that would give two-way access to the spirit world – the Astral Plane, or Hinterland, as Brady had come to think of it. Such access, maintained for only a few minutes each day, had an important function . . .

Brady toured the grounds quickly. The outer layer of defences consisted of a high brick wall, in which was embedded a circle of talismans. These were mosaic tiles from the floor of a very early Roman villa that had once stood where the bottom of his garden now stretched out. The tiles had reverberated with the stored power of fear and death – a brutal event long in the past – when Brady and a friend of his dug them up, making them perfect for the task of defence against psychic attack.

Inside the Talisman Wall was the *zona magnetica*. This was invisible to the naked eye, because the grotesque clay gargoyles with their iron hearts were below the ground. It was a severe barrier to all but the strongest probing or attacking minds. And between the house and the magnetic zone stood the circle of smoking bronze braziers, the *zona mandragora*. These were filled with herbs, roots and chemicals – including various woods, incense and black mandrake – and their organic smoke, produced during their smouldering, was a potent block not just to psychic power, but to any human presence that was radiating such power. The postman could pass through, but a child with a disturbed mind could not.

It was Anita's main task to maintain these defences, the witch's brew in the braziers especially. Brady was very glad of her assistance. Anita's father had been brutally murdered seven months ago, in a remote Norfolk village where Brady had been searching for his daughter. Although her father had actually been a part of the evil force known as Arachne, he had, in a way, been an unwilling victim of that evil. After her grief had subsided,

32

Anita had sought Brady out, to offer her help in any capacity.

Brady did not abuse that offer. The girl lived in Brook's Corner, did housework and, most importantly, maintained the defences. It gave Brady more time to search, and helped him become more organised in the searching.

He was glad, too, of the more intimate arrangement between them, an arrangement which, whilst demanding in certain ways, was maintained without commitment.

The act of sex, a friend of his had once told him, was an incredibly useful defence against psychic attack; *the act of love, emotionally committed and physically enthusiastic, may tire the muscles, but it strengthens the body. Two people who make love vigorously strengthen their individual auras for up to seven or eight hours . . .*

Anita, in a much quieter way than Brady, wanted vengeance for her father's murder. She was prepared to support Brady in any way he needed, knowing that he would soon be the agent of that vengeance.

The final part of the daily morning ritual, undertaken when he was in residence at Brook's Corner and not out in the country following up a clue or hint as to the whereabouts of his family, was to consult the friend who had helped him build the defences, and who had advised him on the role of sex in resisting psychic attack.

Her name was Ellen Bancroft, a young American woman whose family, like Brady's, had been abducted by Arachne. Brady had helped her find her son. Her husband was still lost.

Ellen was a permanent resident at Brook's Corner, and was prepared to remain there until such time as she ceased to be of use to Brady. She could often warn him of impending attack, and was very efficient at driving off unwanted strangers. And because of what she was – a woman existing half way between the earthly plane and the realm of the dead – she could often see things, or become aware of things, that could help Brady in his search for his family and the people who had taken them.

That was why, for a few minutes every day, the

powerful defences around Brook's Corner were opened, allowing spiritual contact with the world outside . . .

Ellen was no material presence in the house: she was a ghost, a spirit which had opted to remain in the fabric of stone and earth that formed the core of the old building. She was cold, she was afraid, she was in pain. The need to pass on into the Hinterland was strong. But she had made it clear to Brady that she would resist that final journey until he felt he could do without her.

Brady loved her for that.

His breakfast finished, Brady went back into the lounge and walked over to the dining-table where paper and pencils lay in orderly piles. Psychic writing was his main method of communication with the fleeting spirit of Ellen Bancroft. Usually she made no response. Sometimes she just complained, a fascinating insight into the 'feelings' of a ghost. Recently, she had made brief, curt statements about Anita Herbert. A jealous ghost, Brady called her, amused at the concept. But since the day, three weeks before, that he had brought the ghost's son Justin to see her, Ellen had been the soul of courtesy.

He sat at the table. Anita sat opposite him, watching his face, in case any visual manifestation occurred there (a common happening). He picked up a pencil and held it lightly against a sheet of paper. In the same movement he checked his watch. It would take him an hour to reach Stefan Taber, which would make him half an hour late. Oh well. If Taber was anything like the usual young person who advertised his psychic talents, his ego would be hurt, but his need for kudos would keep him in angry agreement to wait for a client.

Almost immediately Brady touched pencil to paper, his hand was taken over by the hovering spirit presence of Ellen Bancroft. His pencil traced a series of zig-zags, then a swirl of half-formed letters. Then stopped.

He waited, frowning. The last time this had happened it had been an expression of Ellen's terror and sadness at having made a tentative contact with her son. After Brady had found Justin and brought him home to his mother,

34

he had sent him on, to be cared for by other members of his family. Had Ellen now contacted her husband, Michael?

Anita watched Brady's trembling fingers, her face widely alert with surprise and perhaps excitement.

'There's something up,' she whispered.

Brady hushed her. 'Let her speak without prompting.'

Still the weird stillness persisted, and yet Brady knew that not all was well with the ghost of Ellen Bancroft. There was no point in pushing for a response, either by thinking or speaking any form of question. The bizarre relationship between man and spirit was sufficiently well established by now that each could trust the other to communicate urgency in a straightforward way. (Brady often wondered how his own expressions of grief, or joy, or concern, were comprehended by the ephemeral presence in his house. Perhaps Ellen found it as difficult to understand him as he found it – sometimes – to understand her!)

As he had expected, a moment or two after his blank-minded silence his hand wrote a continual sequence of words, and the words comprised two names: Justin and Michael. They flowed as a confused slash across the paper, and ended with: *Michalmichalmikkkellmi –*

Her joy and frustration expressed, there was the briefest of pauses, and then:

Dan. Ohdan. DAN findhimfindhimfindhim – coldsocold – danDAN – time goingtime – GOING.

Journey – longjourneyfrightenedIfrightened – sofrightened – FRIGH – Calling to meColdcoldcold – timesoon to go. SoongosoonGo –

Moon is coming. The mooncomingiscoming. MOON – comingohDanDANGER – themooniscominghereherehere –

The final pencil-stroke across the paper ended in a crudely drawn circle with an inverted V slashed across it.

Brady stared at the symbol. A circle for the moon, he supposed. But the trisecting lines? 'Why is there danger in the moon?' he asked aloud, but his hand remained still, although the room seemed to quiver a little, as if shuddering with cold.

'Where is the moon coming from? Why is it dangerous? Ellen, can you see anything more?'

After a few seconds his fingers tingled and the pencil slowly and carefully wrote the single word *dark*.

'Keep trying,' Brady whispered. He looked at Anita, who straightened up. 'I want you to stay here . . .'

'Oh no, Dan. I'd like to meet this Taber person!'

'Another time. I want you to stay and keep watch. Keep the channel across the zones open for two hours more. No longer than that. But watch the signalling boxes. If that ash starts to ripple, close the *mazon* immediately. In fact, close it if you feel the slightest tremor or twinge of discomfort.'

Anita nodded. She knew the routine by now.

'Have you had a good breakfast?' Brady asked.

'I'll eat something more. And no alcohol. I know.'

'I should hope not, at this time of the morning.'

She smiled with mock sweetness, then said, 'Be careful.'

'What of? Ghosts on top of the British Telecom Tower? Not unless they take the elevators, and I've never yet heard of a haunted elevator.'

They walked to the front door together. Anita said, 'Then good luck. I hope Taber manages to locate something.'

'If by "something" you mean Alison,' Brady said, kissing the girl on the cheek, 'So do I . . .'

The moon is coming . . .

Danger . . .

As Brady drove rapidly towards the motorway into London, Ellen's cryptic message nagged at him. What could she possibly have seen, peering dimly from the house into the realm of the afterlife, that had reminded her of the moon? Was the word 'moon' some sort of code or image? Was it a *man* with the surname of 'Moon'? Or had

36

she meant that, with a full moon due in a few days, there was a sense of danger occurring on that night?

Well, if *that* was the case, Brady couldn't understand the urgency. Always, when the moon was full, there was danger. Psychic attack was more potent from lunar-influenced minds; supernatural creations could draw upon the odd qualities of moon-reflected sunlight, using it to strengthen their transient life-auras and orientate themselves, rather as pigeons use magnetism to find their way back to home. Brady didn't understand the way moonlight worked; when he left Hillingvale, where all manner of paranormal phenomena were being studied, he had attended a single seminar with the group which was working on a possibly rational basis for the link between lunar reflectivity and cerebellar (hindbrain, the primitive part) activity.

When the moon was up he was always cautious to a maximum, never overestimating his own power, or underestimating the power of *any* attack, however weak that attack might appear.

By the time he reached the motorway, pushing the Land-Rover to a comfortable eighty miles per hour and remaining alert for police patrol cars, the worry about Ellen's lunar message had faded. He began to think, now, of what might be in store for him, two thirds of the way up the British Telecom Tower, where a young medium called Stefan Taber would already be waiting impatiently for him.

He had never met Taber. He knew a little about him by reputation, and he understood that the man had participated in controlled experiments both at Hillingvale and at the Ennean Institute for Paranormal Research. Taber had made two television appearances, both on chat shows, and it was clear that he recognised there was money to be made in his talent . . . or his ability to trick.

But he came to Dan Brady on the recommendation of Brady's close friend and one-time colleague, Andrew Haddingham. Haddingham was now second in command at Hillingvale, and he kept his ears to the ground and his eyes open on behalf of Brady. Brady's job was as secure as any Civil Service job could be; when he was ready to return to work, Haddingham would pull strings. He had pulled many such strings already: Brady was paid free-lance money for doing . . . well, nothing. Brady's savings had run out over the summer. Anita Herbert – on a stipend from the family estate – contributed to the upkeep of house and man, but it was not enough. Haddingham's unofficial hand-outs were very welcome.

Haddingham, knowing of Brady's need for contacts with unusual powers, had been screening such people for months. There was always a danger that talented individuals had already been recruited by Arachne, which had spun its web of evil and destruction across all of England, and probably Europe too. Haddingham was risking life and soul to help his friend. He used Brady's watch, or his signet ring, and sometimes the skull talisman that Brady wore around his neck, to see what those psychically aware people could see with their *mind's* eye.

Stefan Taber had given an astonishing account of Brady's nightmare, seeing details of the girl, Marianna, throwing snowballs at him, reconstructing the account of the attack in vivid detail. All that from a ten-second contact with the watch which Brady had been wearing at the time of his family's abduction. Taber's skill was scan-locating: being able to get an impression of where a body, or an object, was hidden.

That, now, was exactly what Brady needed.

Somewhere in or near London, his wife Alison was trapped, a prisoner waiting to be used in whatever malign way Arachne had planned for her.

It was a long shot, using Stefan Taber to try to 'sense' her. Taber had suggested the British Telecom Tower. Brady had arranged its use through British Telecom.

It was a long shot . . . but he had started to bank on that shot striking true. As he came within sight of the West End of London, his heart-rate doubled and his mouth went dry. Try as he might, he couldn't hold back the tears of hope that began to surface, unbidden, from the still-soft part of the body which fear and horror had hardened.

Thirty-five minutes later than arranged, Brady arrived in the reception area at the base of the British Telecom Tower. He had parked nearby, on a yellow line, deciding to take the chance. Two security men were waiting for him as he stepped through the door; they checked his credentials, then ushered him deeper into the building.

In an armchair across the room, a sallow-faced, blond-haired youth sat reading *Psychic News*. He wore white jeans, white shoes and a white silk shirt. On the left pocket of the shirt an eye had been embroidered.

Brady walked over to him. Stefan Taber looked up, smiled, then carefully folded the paper before rising to his feet. Brady got quite a shock. The man could hardly have been more than five feet four inches tall. His eyes were small and narrow, and his cold grey gaze flickered quickly over Brady as the men shook hands

'I apologise for being late,' Brady said.

'Please don't,' Taber said, smiling superciliously. 'I had a feeling about it.'

'Oh,' Brady said, disappointed at so clichéd a line. 'Really.'

Taber laughed. 'I can't read at home, Mr Brady –'

'Call me Dan.'

'Dan. I can't read in my poky little pad, so I always like an excuse to catch up on the quacks.' He waved the slim paper. 'I *did* feel that you would be late. But that's fine. Did you know that there's a woman in Barnet who has a bottle of condensed ectoplasm?'

Taber chuckled, took Brady by the arm in a very familiar way, and guided him towards the elevator. The security men followed, hands in pockets, one of them smiling slightly. Brady said, 'Ectoplasm? You're kidding.'

Taber shrugged. 'Just when you thought it was safe to attend a seance, all the old rubbish comes up again.'

The lift lurched into motion. One of the security men said, 'Regulations require us to accompany you to the outside platform. Is that going to interfere with what you're up to?'

He addressed Brady, who shrugged. 'It's not going to worry me. This is the man with the power.'

Taber looked up at the Telecom man. 'I'll be fine. I need silence and a promise not to rescue me if you think I'm going to commit suicide. I assure you I won't be. But psychic contact can be distressing.'

The big man laughed, glancing at his solemn, silent companion. 'You want to jump, you jump. We're here to see no damage gets done.'

'That's very encouraging,' Taber said in his slightly forced educated accent.

'We've had them all here,' the security man interrupted. 'Uri Geller. Matthew Manning. Kristof Peryst. All for publicity. This part of a TV project, is it?'

'No,' Taber said coolly, his gaze never leaving Brady. 'I thought I just asked you for silence.'

The security man reddened slightly with irritation. 'Excuse *me*,' he murmured. But he shut up.

Taber was still staring at Brady in a peculiar way. Now he asked, 'Do you *believe* in my powers?'

'Why do you ask?'

'No reason. Do you believe in my powers?' he repeated.

'Do your powers benefit from reassurance?'

'Certainly not.'

'Then don't worry about it. Just do what you've agreed to do.'

Taber laughed out loud again, but the coldness in his eyes gave the lie to his amusement. The elevator slowed to a stop and the doors opened. The security men stood back, and Brady led the medium out into the bright, very cold landing. 'Most people I meet,' Taber said, 'are either in awe of me, or deeply sceptical. You're just indifferent.'

'Certainly not,' Brady said.

'Then you've had a lot of experience with the psychic.'

Brady couldn't help an inward smile. Oh yes, Mr Taber. How right you are.

It suddenly occurred to Brady that Taber was rattled. He wasn't secure in his talent. He was, in fact, deeply *in*secure. No doubt the variability and unpredictability of his power was very unsettling. On one of the chat shows – Russell Harty's, Haddingham had told him – Taber had become very flustered, although out of the embarrassment of initial failure he had told Harty something so personal, and so essentially unknowable, that the compère himself had become very unnerved.

Taber's talent was raw. He had seen its potential, but he was still *frightened* of what he could do. His initial superciliousness was pure defence. His blatant – almost childish – solicitation of Brady's reassurance was not to reinforce his confidence in his talent, but in some strange way to reassure himself of his *normality*.

The cold place into which they had stepped was the old restaurant lounge, long since closed to the public because of its vulnerability to terrorists (some years before, an IRA bomb had exploded in the place, and what should have been one of London's most thrilling night-spots, the revolving restaurant, was gone scarcely before it had been). The view of London was awe-inspiring. To the north, the dark face of an office building and the bright advertising displays on the offices and studios of London Weekend Television; to the west, Regent's Park looked like nothing so much as a forest. The straight roads leading down to the West End were jammed with traffic, and the southern horizon was a distant confusion of white buildings and office towers, with the dome of St Paul's an impressive and instantly recognisable part of the skyline.

Brady felt giddy as he leaned forward and looked at the drop-away, several hundred feet to the street below. Taber was exhilarated by the experience, circling quickly around the window line, familiarising himself with every detail of the view. The whole tower shook slightly, a tremor of shock that made Brady brace himself. He felt slightly foolish, then, as neither Taber nor the security men had seemed to notice the movement. The two Telecom guardians were staring at the view, hands in pockets.

Taber, having completed his circuit, came back to Brady and drew a deep breath.

'Impressive.'

'Terrifying,' Brady agreed.

Taber was staring at him peculiarly. 'It's a huge city, Dan. I don't know that I can scan all of it. I don't even know if I can scan as far as I can see.'

'Do your best,' Brady said. He tried not to think too hard about the simple fact of London's vastness. All he knew was that Alison was in or near London. What an immense area that covered. And yet, as he stared out across the rooftops and gardens, he felt a chill in his bones, and a nagging sense of certainty that she *was* here; somewhere; close by in real terms, close enough to see, close enough to reach in a few minutes . . .

Taber *had* to be able to narrow the search area. If he could successfully locate two corpses, one of them twenty feet below the ground, surely he could scan-locate a living, screaming, desperate woman!

'Did you bring the picture?'

Taber's calm words snapped Brady out of his sudden morbid reverie. He nodded quickly, and reached into his jacket pocket for the photograph of Alison. Taber took it and stared at it for a long time.

'A very beautiful woman,' he said.

'Yes.'

'Is this a recent photo?'

'About eighteen months old. Her hair was shorter the last time I saw her.'

'That doesn't matter,' Taber said. 'Was she pleased with the picture? Did she like it?'

Brady wasn't sure. 'I think so. She wasn't one of those fussy people who hate every picture of themselves. She liked this because I adored it.'

'Where was it kept, when you and Alison were together?'

'In the bedroom . . .'

'Excellent. The picture has a strong resonance, but there *is* a lot of maleness in it. That's you. You've stared at the image a great deal. But so did she. She's there too. It's a *good* picture. It's strong.'

As he spoke, so Taber ran his forefinger lightly over the

42

defined features of Alison Brady, touching lips, eyes, nose, breast. It was an intimate action and Brady, watching the medium carefully, felt oddly disturbed.

He remembered, then, that Taber had asked him to bring a piece of Alison's favourite clothing. He reached into his pocket for the small red silk scarf that Alison had often worn. It was patterned with Chinese ideographs. Brady could hardly bear to look at it; there were many memories associated with the scarf.

'Is this of any use?'

Taber took the delicate item, unfurled it, and manipulated it with his fingers. 'Oh yes. Wonderful. Absolutely wonderful. She wore this a lot, I think. She regarded it as very precious.'

'Yes. She did.'

Taber looked up at him. 'I think I have enough. Alison is now a very powerful presence in my mind. If she's close by, then I'm confident that I can locate her.'

'She may be heavily guarded.' Brady said.

Taber frowned. 'Do you mean . . . what, psychically guarded?'

'I mean exactly that.'

'That would pose problems. I've only come against a psychic barrier twice in my life, and in both cases they were very feeble.'

'The people who have Alison are not feeble,' Brady said quietly.

'Arachne . . .' Taber said, almost nervously, his tone of voice suggesting that he was unsure whether or not to mention the name in front of the other man.

'Had you heard of them before agreeing to help me?' Brady asked, but the psychic shook his head, gazing at Brady in a concerned way.

'Your friend Doctor Haddingham quizzed me at some length about that very thought,' he said. 'You're obviously afraid that anyone at all with paranormal powers might somehow be involved with your wife's abductors.'

It was true. Brady had resolved, months ago, to take chances with nothing, to lack caution at no time . . . to

43

assume that no one was faithful to him, or true . . . save for Andrew Haddingham.

He needed Haddingham, and he needed the trust he felt in the man. It was a small price to pay for sanity's sake.

'You must forgive my nervousness,' Brady said. 'But as far as I know, most people associated with Arachne look, sound and seem quite normal . . . in everyday life.'

'Not the Collectors, though,' Taber said, and Brady frowned.

'Did you get that from touching my watch?'

Taber seemed slightly pleased with himself. They had started to walk towards the stairwell, the Telecom men in tow. They had to get outside, onto the servicing ramp which ran around the tower just above the restaurant level.

'I experienced your nightmare at second hand,' Stefan Taber said quietly, 'and it was damn near as vivid as my own dreams. I've felt I've known Alison for several weeks. I can feel your grief, and your terror. I'm sorry, in a way. It's a very intimate knowledge to share with you. I've been feeling apprehensive about meeting you ever since.'

'I don't mind,' Brady said. 'It told Haddingham that you had a genuine power, a real talent.'

'It's a talent I hadn't fully suspected,' Taber cut in. 'It's hard enough living with feelings of *where* people are, seeing images out of the blue, hearing voices, getting fixations with *water,* or *cellars,* or *woodland.* Suddenly to see the horror that you experienced, those men in their animal masks, the destructiveness . . . and to feel the pain . . . and not to understand what was meant by it all, by Arachne . . .' The young psychic seemed to shiver. His pallid skin was even paler, his lips nervously moist. 'I suppose what's most frightening is the realisation that this Arachne thing really does exist.' As they stepped through a heavy door into the daylight again, Taber glanced at Brady. 'Are they like witches? Black magicians?'

Brady nodded. 'That and more. Whatever their final purpose is, they are using all of magic, and have paranormal talents in all areas. Oh, Jesus!'

His expletive came because of his sudden orientation.

The air was cold and the tower swayed slightly. They were exposed on its side, protected from falling by a chest-high fence, but the ramp was very thin and very narrow, and the wind tugged at him and made him feel like falling. The Telecom men stepped out after them, but both seemed as apprehensive of the exposed height as Brady was.

Only Stefan Taber seemed indifferent to the vertiginous effects of being outside, hundreds of feet above London. He had closed his eyes and was making a slow circuit of the tower again, breathing deeply, and occasionally holding up his left hand, palm flat, as if feeling the view. Twice, as he shuffled around the wind-torn catwalk, he sucked his breath in sharply, as if with shock, hesitating for a moment before continuing. On both of those occasions his hand was reaching out towards the north, beyond Kentish Town and Camden. Those were not parts of London with which Brady was familiar.

At last the height, and the sense of insecurity, became too much for Brady. His knees were wobbling violently, and his stomach was a hard painful knot of tension. His anxiety surfaced in a sudden minor explosion of irritation with the white-clad psychic.

'What the hell are you doing?'

Taber lowered his arm, and turned slowly to face the other man. He was ashen-faced, and his eyes were watering, so that glistening streaks of tears lined the sides of his nose. His expression of anger turned rapidly to a weary sigh of exasperation, then he laughed thinly.

'Go inside, if you want. It would probably be better.'

'But what's with all this feeling? Are you trying to reach out and touch Alison?'

For a moment Taber's face darkened, his eyes narrowing. He wasn't yet ready to reveal what contact he had made, but then decided that perhaps he should. 'That's exactly what I'm doing,' he whispered. 'In fact, it's exactly what I've done . . .'

And as he spoke so he held out the open palm of his hand to Brady, who winced with shock. The man's hand was violently red, the palm raised up in a single, huge blister, which looked as if it would burst around the edges at any time. Dark blue, and pulsing red, coloured the distended skin, and as Brady stared at the weal, so he recognised the crude shape of a face, eyes, nose and mouth picked out in hideous lividity.

'My God,' he whispered. 'Does it hurt?'

'It itches,' Taber said.

'Does this always form? An image of the person you're looking for? Just from contact with a photograph?'

Edging past Brady, and making the catwalk vibrate ominously, Taber said, 'This develops only when I make a contact. She's out there, Dan. You were right. But she's a long way from here . . . I can sense her, but only just . . .'

Brady's heart raced. *She was out there*! The horse-masked Collector, those few weeks before when he had last confronted Arachne, had not lied! She was out there . . . a long way off, but closer than she had ever been before, because now Brady had a starting place, a first step to find her.

They came to the part of the tower that faced north.

'She's there, somewhere,' Taber said, and as he spoke he reached out his arms, widened them slightly, and in so doing encompassed a vast arc of the city, from the north-west to the north-east. 'I'm sorry, Dan. I can't be more specific than that.'

Brady stared into the distance, at the traffic crawling down Hampstead Road and along Euston Road, at the endless vista of rooftops stretching away and up the hills that surrounded central London.

'Nothing more?' he asked quietly. The wind tugged at his hair and jacket, and he clung to the high safety rails with passion.

Taber said, 'A feeling of dark . . . and damp, very damp. No pain, but great tiredness. A silvery light, a bright silver light in the darkness. A noise, like water. Running water, Warm. Dark. Damp. Silver . . . No pain. Just tired . . .' He gripped the rail hard, crying out as he pressed the ferocious blister on his left hand.

'What's the matter?' Brady asked, anxious that some

other image was impinging on the beacon of mind-power that was now Stefan Taber's consciousness.

'Something . . . coming . . .' the medium gasped, and sweat began to pour from his face. Brady noticed that the man's hands were white at the knuckles, that his thin physique was taut and bulging with strained muscles, as if he were hanging on for dear life. His lips were drawn back in agony, and his breath became a series of shallow, shrill gasps.

'*What* is it?' Brady shouted, and began to feel the wind grow stronger, its sound becoming an eerie howling. He glanced to the north and saw a strange black pall, like smoke, hovering over the rooftops of a small area.

'Get . . . in . . .' Taber gasped, and tried to step sideways, reaching slowly along the railings with one hand. His eyes were closed, his face soaked, his silk shirt dark with wetness.

'What can you feel?' Brady screamed at him. 'Is it Alison?'

Was she being killed? Is that what he could sense, that the woman with whom he was in contact was now being slaughtered? Come on, Taber, speak to me, what is it, *what* is it, what can you see?

'Help me!' the psychic screamed suddenly, and his left hand shot out towards Brady, who took an involuntary step backwards. The whole hand was a grotesque balloon, a red and yellow swollen mass, the fingers mere pudgy, udder-like extensions of the bulging palm. It pulsed and changed colour to a vile blue-black as Brady stared at it in horrified fascination.

On the other side of the racking, screaming shape of Stefan Taber, one of the security men was standing, watching in similar horror. A moment later the man turned and fled back to the access door into the tower.

'*Reaching* . . .!' came Taber's almost incoherent screech. Brady stepped away from him, then looked to the north . . .

From the dark pall of smoke a thin tendril of dark was curling towards the tower, moving like a high-speed train. Simple survival instinct sent Brady scurrying further away

.rom the psychic, and a second later the finger of darkness wrapped itself about the shuddering man.

The air about Brady became grey, as if in a storm. His body was not so much tugged as *sucked* against the safety railings. Taber's body was slammed forwards and backwards, and though he raised his arms to protect himself, he was gripped too tightly, and was being thrashed so hard against the metal that his bones were cracking.

The wind was a mournful moaning, and above it, chillingly close, was the baying of a hound, or a wolf . . .

And the face of that hound emerged from the gloom, its jaws open and slavering, its eyes glowing red. It snapped at Taber. Taber screamed. It wrenched at the rails, and the metal bent outwards. Taber's body was suddenly snatched from the catwalk. It hovered in mid-air for a brief moment, as it was shaken and worried by the huge spectral animal face, and then was flung out of Brady's view, across the rooftops, to smash into the crowds below.

As quickly as it had come, the thread of dark, with its ghostly hound, was sucked back into the distance.

Brady watched it go; saw where it vanished.

In the few minutes before the police came, Brady crossed the road from the tower's base and fetched his *A to Z* of London from the Land-Rover. One of the security men went with him, the one who was deeply shaken by what had happened, the one who had said to Taber to go ahead and jump, all they were there for was to see that no bombs got planted. The other Telecom man went across to the forecourt of the LWT building, where the bloody and broken corpse of Stefan Taber lay, covered with a canteen table-cloth.

On the *A to Z* Brady marked a line from the tower to the place where he had seen the dark cloud. He couldn't be precise. But it gave him a start. In his mind he held an idea – that Alison was guarded and the guardian – in a single, explosive burst of power – had destroyed the probing mind of the medium. The area of dark had not been as close as Mornington Crescent, but could well have been from Camden Town or beyond.

It would still be a frustratingly difficult search.

The police came. They took statements and checked the damage to the British Telecom Tower railings. The body had been flung four hundred yards, but there was no evidence of a bomb blast. Brady gave the name of Andrew Sutherland, a detective-superintendent on the Thames Valley Force who was aware of what had happened to Brady, and of the likelihood of bizarre occurrences being associated with him.

At two in the afternoon, Brady was allowed to drive home.

At three, as he turned into a country road just a few minutes from Brook's Corner, he thought he heard – above the sound of the engine – the throaty barking of a dog. In his rear-view mirror a dark shape fleetingly passed through his vision, vanishing into the pinewoods at the roadside.

He slowed the vehicle and looked back along the road, but there was nothing to be seen except for a Securicor van.

He drove on slowly, and soon came in sight of the house.

3

Something killed Tip . . . and it's gonna kill you too . . .

Her words, horribly prophetic, came back to haunt
Pippa Thompson as she scampered through the grey
streets, following closely behind her brother. Flynn had
taken the lead as usual, and was waving her back, then
beckoning her forward as he led them on a zig-zagging
route around the area, making for their first place of safety.

Both children were totally unnerved by the experience
in the wasteland. Where Ritchie Hughes had gone they
didn't know. The last Flynn had seen of him he had been
streaking away to the south, head low, arms pumping. He
had been heading for home.

But Errol Flynn Thompson was nervous of pursuit.
The way that dog had stopped and stared at them, so quiet,
so calm, as if memorising their faces . . .

As if waiting for its mistress to catch up with it before
continuing the pursuit.

Ultimately, they would *have* to go home. Only at home
could he be sure of finding the right marks, and words, to
keep the nightmare dogs at bay. He had seen the hex book,
the *hunganzi* book, as the adults called it, hidden in his
parents' bedroom. In *hunganzi* was their protection. In the
book was their only insurance against being killed liked
Gerry.

But first they would have to put the hounds off the
track. Hence the exaggerated and complex route home,
darting towards, then away from, the location of their
house, making steadily for Airbase 50 behind the garages,
where the old allotments were overgrown and there were a
hundred hiding-places.

Pippa kept crying. She would get angry, then cry again.

Flynn felt like crying too, at the image of Gerry Cronin burning silver, and the way that phantom dog had snapped out his throat . . . Flynn would have liked nothing better than to run home, screaming to his mother to save them. But they had got themselves into this mess and they would have to get themselves out. There was something in Flynn that was terrified of inviting the danger home. His parents could always have more children, he had said to himself, bullying himself into responsibility, but he and Pippa could never have more parents.

'Come *on*,' he snapped at the girl, who was limp and tired as she trotted along behind him, her anorak flapping open.

'Let's go home,' she said. 'I'm frightened.'

'Not for an hour. Maybe two. It's too dangerous.'

'I *know*,' the girl protested. 'That's why I want to go home. I want to hide in my room. I'm *scared*, Flynn. I don't want no big dog biting me. I don't like dogs . . .'

Flynn hushed her with a firm hand over her mouth. But he smiled, then rapidly scanned the streets behind them. Taking his sister's hand, he dragged her on. 'Not far to go . . .'

He took her behind the low warehouses, where men in stained overalls worked on half-wrecked cars; then into the street, where the houses were half empty and half fallen down; then to the garages, where more kids and youths tinkered with their dream machines. Flynn cautiously led the girl to the broken fencing, squeezed through and rearranged the slats.

They went to the deserted and ramshackle garden-shed which was their Control Centre for Airbase 50. There they sat, huddled together, for more than an hour.

From Airbase 50, Flynn led his reluctant sibling to Fort Alpha. He half expected to find Ritchie Hughes there, but the place was deserted and the message wall was blank. Fort Alpha was an abandoned house, its doors and windows barricaded with boards, its floors almost all fallen in. The access to this place of decay and debris was through a broken cellar window. But the place smelled so badly of cats, and other things more rotten, that after a few minutes Flynn decided it was time to go home and get the book from his parents' bedroom.

It was now or never. Pippa was delighted. She stopped whining and did what she was told.

It was mid-afternoon.

Their home was a small, brightly painted terrace house. The back garden was meticulously laid out and well looked after. The small greenhouse, where exotic plants grew, formed a perfect screen for their cautious approach towards the back door.

Flynn slipped in first, then Pippa. Their father was at work. He was station-master at a Northern Line tube-station, and cycled several miles there and back. He would not return until the evening. Mrs Rosamund Thompson, their mother, was busy repairing a tear in her white coat, the one she wore to church on Sundays and which was an inheritance from her own mother.

Rosamund looked up as the kids sneaked past to the base of the stairs. She had heard a slight sound, but then dismissed it. She was young and very athletic-looking, keeping herself fit on the tracks at the White Hart Lane sports centre. She worked part-time as a secretary, and most of the time as a disciplinarian for her two errant children. Born in the West Indies, she had come to England when less than a year old and had no feeling at all for the 'back-home place'. Husband John, however, was from an old and well-respected island family. He had arrived in England as a boy of six, not knowing that his father was a Baron, a *hungan* or dark priest of great renown. When his father had died, the dry parchment papers that formed the *hunganzi*, the book of power and wisdom, had passed to John.

He was the guardian of the book. There were many such in the broadly spread and extensive West Indian population of London.

Rosamund was singing quietly to herself. Flynn took a step on the stairs, then froze as he heard his mother get up from her chair. But she went into the kitchen and water ran noisily into a saucepan. The children took the opportunity and nipped up the stairs.

The landing was dark. Pippa opened the door to her room, and light spilled from the open window. All she wanted to do was to go in, lock the door and crawl under the bedcovers, but Flynn shook her arm, dragging her to the big room at the end.

He opened the door to their parents' bedroom and stepped quickly inside. They had always been forbidden to enter without specifically being invited. On Sunday mornings they would all gather on the big double bed and drink tea and eat toast fingers, before getting ready for church. But apart from that treat, the room was out of bounds.

The curtains were closed, the room in semi-darkness. From the walls, the faces of the dead and of the living-but-far-away peered solemnly at the children. All the photographs were framed in glass, and light gleamed faintly from each of them.

The room was a veritable museum of times past and times present. On the chest of drawers stood wooden statues, exquisitely dressed dolls, vases, patterned china and silver-backed brushes and combs. On shelves around the walls were books, metal objects, old guns and rusting knives. There were paintings of seascapes, villages and people. Where the wall was not covered with images, coloured beads hung in long strands. The whole place had a funny smell, slightly perfumed but sharp. Sometimes, at church, the same smell drifted past, but stronger. It was a sort of incense smell, but it made Flynn dizzy, and it made Pippa feel sick.

They tip-toed about the dim room, gently opening drawers to expose the tightly packed, neatly folded clothes. Pippa suddenly whispered, 'What's it look like, this funny book?'

'Like a book,' Flynn whispered back. 'It's got leather covers, and it's held together by string . . .' He said 'string', even though he knew that the binding was dried cockerel gut. 'It smells funny . . .'

'Don't everything,' Pippa said pointedly.

Flynn had seen his father leafing through the book just once. His father had been outside the room, and another man had been standing with him. Flynn had watched from his own bedroom. He had learned the name of the book, and the fact that it contained charms, hexes, blocking spells and words of wisdom. The man with John Thompson had wanted to warn off an evil eye. He had been given a dried animal's foot and some funny herbs, and was memorising some nonsense words.

From that moment – a year ago – Flynn had looked with new eyes at the dingy, crowded bedroom. The dried head of a rooster hung just inside the door. Each wall had a small black symbol on it: two entwined snakes. Above the bed hung a peculiar cross, made out of iron, with the letters B and S marked on the cross-piece, and the face of a monkey scratched out on the top.

These were all magic things from the back-home place. There were other marks and symbols in the room, and small eyes with snakes running through them were marked in every room in the house. And Flynn knew that below a floorboard in his bedroom – and probably Pippa's too – there was something soft wrapped up in muslin, a little bag painted black that he had never dared open and examine.

All of these things were simple protections, just as Gerry Cronin's house had dishes of Holy Water everywhere, and images of Jesus with his heart exposed, and Holy Mary in her blue robe, her hands raised in a hex warning.

But Flynn knew that these protections were against weak things. The black dogs and the hag-like image of the old woman were not weak. He had heard his father tell someone that when ghosts started to haunt a body, there would always be an answer in the *hunganzi* book.

How he hoped his father was right.

At last he found the bound sheets of parchment. They were under the mattress, wrapped up in black muslin and covered by a black sheet below the thick feather overlay.

54

He unwrapped the book almost nervously, while Pippa watched him, goggle-eyed and scared.

When Flynn finally held the ancient book a strange feeling of power coursed through him. His head, muzzy with the smell of the incense or whatever it was, cleared suddenly. Though the room was gloomy, he suddenly saw everything in it very clearly. The leather was cold and cracked. The whole binding was heavy. The dried gut that stitched the sheets together had an uncanny, living feel about it. When he opened the book, touching the dry, brittle parchment, he was almost shocked at the way the ink-drawn symbols and words moved with an illusory life of their own.

'Come on,' he whispered to Pippa, and replaced the bedclothes carefully. Then, with the precious hex book under his arm, he led the way to his room, creeping quietly across the landing.

Not quietly enough.

'Who's there?' Rosamund called from downstairs. Pippa slapped a hand to her mouth, but Flynn just shook his head, frowning at her, indicating to her that she should not be so jumpy. 'We're on a practice escape session,' he whispered, and she understood.

'That you, Errol?' their mother called again. She had come to the bottom of the stairs. 'Pippa?'

Pippa walked out of the room and mimed to her mother to be quiet.

'What's up, child? I didn't hear you come in.'

'We came in through the window,' Pippa whispered. 'It's an escape practice. Ritchie Hughes is out the front, waiting for us.'

'Ritchie? He can come in if he wants . . .'

'*Training* session,' Pippa whispered urgently.

Rosamund laughed. 'You and those comics. Is Errol with you?'

'Yes.'

'Well, that's good. You remember what I told you, now . . .'

'Keep together,' Pippa said.

'That poor McGeary boy should've known better, and I don't want you or Errol walking about on your own. You remember what time I want you back tonight?'

'Five o'clock.'

'And not one minute later. Your daddy and me have got a very important meeting tonight, and I want you washed, fed and round at the Hughes' place by seven.'

From his room, where he had the *hunganzi* book opened on his bed, Flynn looked up in alarm. He'd forgotten that they were being looked after by Mr and Mrs Hughes tonight. The idea was frightening. Ritchie wouldn't have taken any precautions, and if he *had* gone straight home, and if the dogs had followed him . . .

He stared at the yellow parchment. He could hardly understand any of what was written and drawn there. *To turn about a jinga. To turn about a bat eye or night wing. To stop a grave earth. To draw spirit from a loa. The veve.*

Frantically, he turned the pages. So many of the words were funny words, foreign words. They were probably African, or magic, and he didn't recognise any of them. He had not thought of this, that the book of voodoo wisdom would be mostly written in a secret code that only the *hungan* would understand.

Then, just as Pippa came back into the room, looking worried and edgy, he found something useful.

Pippa said, 'Put it back now, Flynn. It's too risky . . .'

'Wait . . .' he said, and ran his finger along the line of words. 'Look. *To turn about grey hag.*' He looked up at his sister. 'You didn't see it, but there was an old woman with the dogs. Ritchie called her an old hag.'

Pippa was shaking with nerves. She waved her hand, indicating that she didn't care about all that. 'Just write it down, then, and put the book back. Write it down . . .'

Flynn quickly copied out the several symbols that were drawn on the page, then copied the funny words carefully. He looked on the back of the sheet, but there was just the representation of a dead man's face, the tongue hanging out, the eyes blind. He closed the *hunganzi* book and

56

wrapped the black cloth around it again. Tip-toeing along the landing, he entered the main bedroom and replaced the book below the mattress.

Quickly, he took down the cockerel's head from where it hung behind the door and placed it in his pocket. In the bottom drawer of the wardrobe were hundreds of small bottles, all neatly labelled, and he searched through them rapidly until he found one labelled 'manjooza'. This was the only word he had recognised from the page on 'turning about a grey hag'. Manjooza was animal blood – or perhaps man's 'juice' – and in its dried and powdered state it was very effective in warding off evil spirits.

With these two purloined items, Flynn crept back to his own room. He found a thick piece of charcoal and dipped the end of it in the manjooza. The first mark he made on the wall was dull red, but the rest of the symbol that he inscribed there was a smudgy black. He marked all four walls, the ceiling and the floor with the stopping spells. He had no idea if he was doing the right thing. He copied the strange words on a sheet of an exercise book and folded it under his pillow.

Pippa watched him, her small body trembling. 'Hurry up,' she whispered. 'If Mum catches us . . .'

'She won't. Read out these words with me.'

Standing in the middle of the room they whispered the words in a dull monotone, slowly turning round in a full circle.

'*Ojum zoobos manjooz samedi kanzo* . . .' they murmured, ritually.

'What's it mean?' Pippa asked.

'Powerful magic.'

'But what do the words mean?'

'If we knew that, they wouldn't work.'

'That's silly.'

'It's the power of voodoo.'

'You don't know. You're making it all up.'

'You saw the words in the *hunganzi* book.'

'Probably a recipe for sweet potatoes.'

'The hag'll get you if you don't believe.'

Pippa shuddered at the thought. 'Do my room now. Come on.'

A few minutes later Flynn had finished the defences in Pippa's room, and no hag-soul or demon-dog would be able to pass through the walls. They hoped. It was the best he could do. The charm, with its words and symbols, had to mean *something*. To turn about a grey hag . . . Yes, Flynn decided; that *was* the right piece of voodoo for the purpose.

The problem now was Ritchie Hughes. Ritchie was in equal danger, and somehow Flynn had to communicate the details of the charm to him. If he and Pippa were going to have to spend the evening in the Hughes' house, Flynn wanted to be sure of some protection there.

'Can I use the phone?' he called to his mother from the hallway.

'Who d'you want to ring?'

'Ritchie.'

'Okay. But be quick. The last bill was twenty pounds, and you know who cost most of that . . .'

Flynn took the phone into the dining-room. He called Ritchie. When the fat boy came on the phone his voice was weak. He sounded as if he'd been crying.

'Ritchie . . . get a pencil and paper . . .'

'Why?' asked the boy miserably.

'You're hexed, man,' Flynn whispered urgently. 'Got to break it. I got the way here.'

'What way?'

'A magic way. I found some charms, some spells. Hurry up, Ritchie.'

Reluctantly, Ritchie Hughes went away and came back with a notepad. Flynn started to describe the symbols, with their twisting snakes, open eyes and crosses. But Ritchie found it too hard to follow. So Flynn settled for spelling out the words and urging his friend to speak them out loud in his room.

He had got as far as 'manjooza' when a hand reached past him and snatched his own notepad from the floor.

'What in the blue blazes are you doing?' his mother said,

58

her voice sounding hushed and shocked. 'Put the phone down. Put it down!'

Flynn obeyed. Rosamund stared at the scrawled words, then looked at him. Flynn stood up slowly. It was hard to tell whether the expression on his mother's face was anger, shock or fear.

'Where d'you get these?' she asked quietly, shaking her head as if in disbelief.

'From a book at school,' Flynn lied.

Rosamund's hand lashed out and caught him a stinging blow round the right ear. 'These aren't from any book at school.'

'A boy brought them in. He said he's seen them at home and they're good for warding off the evil eye.'

'What boy?'

'Don't know his name. A new boy.'

'Black?'

'Yes.'

Rosamund stared at the paper. 'Stay here,' she said. She ran quickly up the stairs and Flynn heard her walking into the main bedroom. From the sounds that came through the ceiling he knew she was checking under the mattress. Pippa appeared quietly in the door to the dining-room, looking wide-eyed and concerned, though the concern was touched with amusement.

Obviously satisfied that all was well with the *hunganzi* book, Flynn's mother went into the children's bedrooms. Her cry and shock and horror was followed by a stern summons upstairs. She was standing in the middle of the room, looking at the large charcoal symbol opposite the door. Flynn shuffled uneasily behind her. She turned round quickly, her face set very grim, and firmly boxed both of his ears.

'You'll get it from your father for doing this,' she said.

'What's the point of a charm if we can't use it,' he muttered, cradling his stinging face.

'*You* don't use a charm *ever*!' his mother said angrily. '*You* don't use it . . . other people use it *for* you. Trained people. Look at all this, Errol Look! It's all wrong. It's

59

bad. You use charms to ward off evil, but if there's no evil to ward off the charm itself can become evil.'

Flynn said despondently, 'But there *is* evil. It's an old hag with black dogs, and she's haunting us . . .'

'I never heard of anything so ridiculous!'

'It's true. It's a ghost, a terrible ghost!'

Rosamund reached out and tapped her son firmly on the head. 'The only ghost is the ghost of your intelligence. In here! Look at all this rubbish . . .' She picked up a handful of comics and waved them at him. 'Pictures, bad language, childish rubbish. It's all you read. Why don't you read some *good* books. Your head's so full of space and guns it's no wonder you're having bad dreams . . .'

'It's not a dream. There *is* a ghost.'

But his mother would have none of it. 'Get washed, then go and sit at the table. I'll take you round to the Hughes' myself, before your father comes home. If you promise to clean these silly marks off the wall, I won't tell him. Go on, now. Go and wash . . .'

An hour later Flynn and Pippa were marched briskly the half mile or so to Ritchie Hughes' house. It was after dusk, and a very chilly night. But Flynn, glancing anxiously around as his mother dragged him on, was cold to his bones, cold with fear.

He had managed to rescue the sheet of paper with the charm symbols on it. He had tucked the sheet inside his briefs, for extra safety.

Ritchie was in a terrible state. Flynn and Pippa were allowed upstairs to his room, and told that there would be tea and biscuits at nine o'clock. Rosamund left with a last angry glance at her two children. As soon as she was out of sight, Flynn drew out the paper sheet and his piece of charcoal and began to 'decorate' Ritchie's room.

The fat boy sat on his bed, huddled up and sweating, his thumb stuck in his mouth. Pippa sat with him, but didn't know what to say. Then Flynn insisted that Ritchie joined in the chanting, and the three children repeated the shuffling circular movement whilst murmuring the words of protection.

For the rest of the evening they sat by the window, with the room lights out, and watched the night, apprehensive for the first gleam of silver.

At ten o'clock the front doorbell was rung. Rosamund Thompson stood there, and a taxi kept its engine running in the road outside. While the adults talked in the hallway, Flynn tried to shake some courage into Ritchie, but the boy just shivered and turned away.

'Stay alert, my guy,' Flynn said, resting his hand briefly on Ritchie's shoulder.

'They're going to get me,' Ritchie muttered. 'I just know it . . .'

Flynn followed Pippa into the taxi. They sat together on the back seat, staring at Ritchie's house. When the taxi moved off they twisted round to stare through the back window. Flynn didn't know what to do for the best. Ritchie had given up, but his room had some basic charm protection. It was no good talking to his parents, because all parents thought was that childish imaginations were running wild . . .

Flynn didn't know what to do for the best!

Then Pippa gasped. Craning in his seat, Flynn followed her pointing finger. The taxi slowed at a junction, then began to pull out to the right. But before the Hughes' house vanished from view, Flynn saw the silvery glow that had suddenly appeared in the distance.

Ritchie went downstairs to get a glass of milk. He walked into the sitting-room, where his parents were watching television. His mother looked round at him and smiled. 'You'll be a tired young man tomorrow. Still, a late night now and then won't hurt you.'

'Going to bed now.'

'Goodnight, dear.'

'Night . . .' said his father.

Ritchie turned away from them and went back to his

room. He tugged on his pyjamas and climbed into bed. He turned the light out, finished off the milk, then sat in the darkness, hugging his knees, watching the closed bedroom door.

Suddenly he sat bolt upright in bed and his eyes widened. He had heard the sound of someone running quickly up the stairs.

A moment later a second person – or an animal – padded swiftly from the hall to the landing. The floorboards outside his room creaked.

'Can't come in . . .' Ritchie whispered. He held up his hand where Flynn had painted the image of an eye. 'Go away. I'm protected,' he said, and raised his voice louder. 'Manjooza . . . er . . . samdi zoobie . . . er . . .' he began to panic. He couldn't remember the words. 'Manjooza . . .' he repeated weakly, and tears began to well up in his eyes.

There was a heavy silence outside the room. Distantly, he could hear the television, a man's voice singing.

Something scratched at the door.

An eerie silver light began to form on the inside of the closed door, coming through the wood, coming through the walls on either side of it . . .

In a sudden panic Ritchie turned on the light, blinking at the brightness. The silvery glow was still there, shifting and drifting like smoke.

Something else . . . a huge round shape, a black shape, pushing into the room through the wood, twisting and turning . . .

A head . . . a dog's head the size of a horse's hind-quarters . . . huge! Suddenly it snarled. The mouth opened in the amorphous black shape, and the great red tongue lolled, the yellowing canines glistening. Then the eyes appeared, glowing, demonic. Then the ears, pricked up and listening. The immense beast stared at him, its head moving from side to side, its breath laboured and loud. A second dog's head, as large as the first, pushed slowly through the wall that connected with his parents' bedroom. The two hounds glared at him, growling deep in their throats.

The television sounded: a burst of applause, followed by a jaunty orchestral number.

Between the heads of the panting mastiffs, the silver light grew to a blinding intensity. It flowed into the room and formed the shape of a woman. Her face was the face of a corpse, her hands long and skeletal, her body a gruesome exhibition of decay glimpsed clearly through the gossamer fabric of the grave robes. When she pointed at him he felt his skin burn. He tried to cry out, for the first time, but the sound choked in his throat. He raised his arms towards her and saw how his skin glowed silver. Fire began to burst from his fingers, and the pain was excruciating. Again he tried to scream, but though his mouth opened, no noise came.

Fire and flame swathed him. Through the agony he saw one of the great dogs squirm all the way through the wall and come towards him. It towered above him, watching, its mouth opened. The pain had gone, and consciousness with it, by the time it leaned down and almost carefully positioned its jaws around his throat . . .

4

There was a car parked on the roadside opposite Brook's Corner. It was not marked as a police car, but Brady recognised it: Detective-Superintendent Andrew Sutherland had come to visit.

Brady had been expecting the policeman but had hoped for a few hours to shake off the shock of Taber's sudden death. He felt unnerved by what had happened – upset would have been too strong a word – and the feeling was exacerbated by the sensation that he was being followed.

By a dog . . . a spectral black dog . . .

He drove into the grounds of his house and locked the Land-Rover. The air was sharp with the smell of burning woodland matter. And a small red ribbon, tied to the sash of the study window, was Anita's discreet warning that all was not well inside . . .

As Brady walked round to the back door, Anita appeared at the kitchen window, raising a finger to her lips and signalling frantically with her eyes. When he stopped and smiled she opened the window and whispered, 'There's a policeman here. That Superintendent Sutherland.'

'I know,' Brady whispered back.

'Something's gone wrong,' she stated bluntly. Her face was pale; she looked anguished.

'Taber's dead.'

'Oh, God. How?'

Brady shrugged. 'Not easy to say at the moment. Where is he?'

'Snooping around in the garden.'

Brady nodded. 'Right . . .' He glanced back at Anita. 'Make me some coffee? It's been a long day.'

'OK. Good luck.' She pulled the window closed.

Brady walked slowly round to the long rear section of the garden where it overlooked some rough ground and a thin line of woodland. For a moment he couldn't see Sutherland and assumed that the policeman had gone back into the house. Then he saw the man, half hidden beyond the apple trees that formed a small orchard at the end of the lawn. Sutherland was crouching at the lip of the shallow excavation, peering at the crudely uncovered marble floor where, until recently, a Roman mosaic had been laid out.

Brady approached quietly. Sutherland rose to his feet after a moment or two, slung his overcoat over his shoulder and walked round the low brick wall, looking into the distance. Brady watched him. The policeman worried at the cement between the bricks with his finger, touched some of the charcoal and chalk symbols that had been scratched there (and which needed constant renewal), then strolled leisurely up the garden. He stood, quite close to Brady, looking down into a smouldering brazier.

After a moment's frowning contemplation, Sutherland reached into the shallow bronze dish and pinched up a sample of the pungent organic material within. He rubbed it between his fingers and sniffed at it, looking slightly perturbed, as if the aroma upset him.

'Mandrake, hellebore and wolfsbane,' Brady said, from where he stood just fifteen yards away, among the apple trees. Sutherland glanced up in surprise, smiling very thinly.

'I didn't see you.'

Brady approached. 'Plus: fragments of three woods, a few crystals of frankincense and something to make it all burn very slowly.'

'Stinks,' the policeman observed. 'Stinks something horrible.'

'Not recommended for flavouring stews,' Brady agreed, and Sutherland laughed, wiping his fingers on a pocket handkerchief.

The man looked older each time Brady saw him. Sutherland was tall and middle-aged, with ice-grey eyes and grey hair, which he combed back very severely, and very close to his skull. His face was ruddy, his lips thin, and when he smiled he looked very warm; when he didn't, he looked very angry, the sort of man who is unreadable, and who might be planning to strike, even though his lips are stretched into a grin. He had encountered Brady on several occasions, and knew the full story of what had happened to Brady's family. He knew about Arachne. He had dealt with other instances of Arachne's 'gathering'. The agreement between the two men – who were both equally lost in this situation – was that in return for a free flow of information, Sutherland would accept that Brady had no *intention* of killing, or causing to be killed, any man or woman who suffered a fatality during his search for his family.

It was a difficult agreement. Brady had said that he would not himself kill anyone. But people tended to end up beneath white sheets whenever Brady was around. It took a great suspension of disbelief on the policeman's part to accept that sometimes people were killed, or attacked, by the *mind*, or by savage creations from a group mind that was dedicated to covering Arachne's tracks.

'Here we go again . . .' Sutherland said, walking up to Brady and staring him straight in the eye.

'So it would seem.'

Sutherland sniffed cautiously at his fingers, and still seemed unhappy. 'What's this gunk for, did you say?'

'Better than garlic or Holy Water for keeping unpleasant forces of the night at bay.'

'Garlic,' the policeman repeated. 'Vampires.' He shook his head, still watching Brady closely. 'Have you encountered a vampire yet?'

'Only Anita Herbert,' Brady said with a quick smile. 'Fifteen years' age difference is . . . well, let's just say quite a difference.'

Sutherland let the wryest of smiles touch his lips. 'Keeps you in trim, does she?'

'Sex is a very effective defence against psychic attack.'

The policeman laughed out loud. 'Is that a fact, now? I

shall have to remember to mention it to a certain colleague at our next weekend special training group.'

There was a chill wind blowing, and the sky was clouding over. Sutherland put on his overcoat again, his face solemn now. 'Every few months,' he said to Brady, 'a death occurs. Did I say a death? Singular? Correction: every few months, bloody *mayhem*.' Brady watched the man impassively. Sutherland buttoned up his coat. 'As a policeman my strongest instinct is to slap you in the slammer. Put you away . . .' he added deliberately, speaking slowly and carefully.

'I'm familiar with the expression,' Brady said.

'But not with the experience, eh?'

'Certainly not.'

Sutherland shook his head, a gesture that imparted much despair to Brady. 'First a burned man and a dead American girl, right here, right in the house. Then farmers and village folk slaughtered in Norfolk, and one young man . . .' Sutherland shivered at the thought. 'One young man strangled by something that oughtn't to have left its grave.' Now his stare hardened, his gaze almost angry. 'And then,' he went on softly, 'I find that you were in the hills between Manchester and Sheffield at about the same time that over eleven people were killed in their beds. You couldn't have been there *and* in Wales, where a hospital's geriatric ward lost all its patients in a single night . . . but I don't know. I'm not sure. I'm not sure of anything any more, least of all . . . you, Mr Brady.'

'A hospital?' Brady said. He knew nothing of the event.

Sutherland nodded. 'A boy says he saw . . . listen to this . . . a Red Indian warrior. Next thing, ten dead men, and two police cars thrown forty yards by a sudden wind.'

A Red Indian warrior!

So the events in Casterigg of last summer, when he had come so desperately close to his daughter Marianna, had been the end of a longer trail of violence . . .*

But he had read nothing in the papers, and the killings in the Peak District town had been very much played

*See *Nighthunter 3: The Ghost Dance*.

down in the nationals. Brady asked Sutherland about this.

'We now have a very understanding relationship with the Press. We have their full co-operation.' He was being slightly cynical. 'What I mean is, we tell them absolutely nothing. If they find out a glimmer of the truth of events, they get a cover story. Hell's Angels. Gas explosions. Crime of passion. The papers are full of lies these days, but until we know what's going on we daren't risk provoking the public imagination.'

'Copy-cat killings and the like, you mean.'

They began to walk slowly towards the house again. Brady could see Anita watching them from the landing window. Sutherland said, 'This Stefan Taber . . . did you know him well?'

'Today was our first meeting.'

'Short and very tragic.'

'I didn't expect it to be that way.'

'He was a medium . . . .'

'A psychic,' Brady agreed. 'I'd asked him to try and scan-locate Alison. You know, get a psychic feeling of her.'

'Like locating a body . . .'

'A living body, in this case.'

Sutherland said, 'Why London?'

'She's hidden there. Somewhere, I'm sure of it.'

'From what you learned at Anerley . . .' Sutherland looked round. 'Another little disaster area.'*

Brady took a deep breath. 'I did my best to preserve life there, to protect the farmers. Most of the mayhem was caused because one of them went over the edge. I suppose I should have seen it. But with each encounter I learn to handle the situations better.'

Sutherland said icily, 'Tell that to Taber's mother.'

Brady remained silent. The policeman went on. 'Did he find her? Did he scan-locate her?'

'Partly.' Brady said. 'He sensed her, but it was a very tentative touch.'

'And he died for the privilege.'

'Was killed for it.'

*See *Nighthunter 4: The Shrine.*

68

'Murder, then.'

'He wasn't the suicidal type,' Brady agreed.

'I'd vaguely wondered about suicide . . .' Sutherland said. 'But my colleagues at the Met are crawling all over the tower looking for evidence of explosion.'

'I'm amazed they let me go,' Brady murmured.

'They're at a loss. Nothing about Taber's death computes. One moment he's hundreds of feet up the side of the British Telecom Tower, and the next he's hitting the pavement four hundred and fifty yards north. Dead. That's one hell of a gust of wind.'

They stopped by the back door and the policeman turned to look at Brady. 'The Met boys . . . they're a nice mob. But a bit slow. A bit inclined to be unimaginative. There's got to be a reason for everything. No gust of wind could have blown a man four hundred yards or more. And you couldn't have thrown him. So a bomb's the only answer. But a bomb that hardly causes any damage or burning? It's got them on the run. So they invoke The Answer. The Answer is that you're lying, that the security officers at the Telecom Tower are lying, and that Taber fell from somewhere else. If it's not a bomb, the AT boys aren't interested in holding you, so you go free. Within a matter of hours the file will be in Room 17.'

Opening the back door, Brady led the way into the house. Percolated coffee steamed quietly on the small kitchen table, and Brady poured two mugs. Sutherland took his black; Brady added a little sugar. As he passed one mug to the policeman he said, 'Room 17. Where's that? Whitehall?'

'New Scotland Yard. Basement. The room that knows. Room 17.'

Sipping his coffee, Brady stared at the other man. Sutherland's ice-cold stare never moved from Brady's face. 'Unexplained death,' Brady guessed, and Sutherland nodded.

'Unexplained anything. It was set up five months ago. It has two desks, two filing cabinets, a computer link and printer, two telephones, one very old coffee-maker. Two men sit there, one a copper the other a parapsychologist. There are three mugs. The third mug is for the portly and very energetic Man from Whitehall. From the Home Office, to be exact. From Room 23. His name is Kotting and he represents the extent to which the Government is beginning to take seriously the occult threat to this country.'

'Well, well,' Brady said quietly. 'And is it directives from Room 17 that have kept me free, and not behind bars?'

Sutherland shrugged. 'Perhaps. Unnatural circumstances demand unnatural measures. Rule bending. But they know about you, now, and about what *you* know.'

'Are they watching me?' Brady led Sutherland through the dark hallway into the bright and airy lounge, where Anita Herbert sat in an armchair, pretending to read a paper.

'No, they're not watching you,' Sutherland said. '*I'm* watching you. If you co-operate with us, telling us what you find out and giving us a chance to prevent any unnecessary unpleasantness . . .'

'As opposed to necessary unpleasantness . . .' Brady said quietly, but Sutherland just shrugged.

'If you co-operate with us, we'll continue to co-operate with you.'

The policeman prowled about the lounge, looking at photographs, pictures, and at the sheets of that morning's psychic writing session with Ellen. He picked up one of the pieces of paper and peered more closely at it as he sipped coffee. Then he murmured. 'The moon is coming.' He glanced at Brady. 'What's this?'

'The results of a seance,' Brady said, deliberately obfuscating the truth.

'Mean anything?'

'Not yet.'

Sutherland put the paper and his mug down and walked slowly back to Brady. He sat down on the arm of the sofa and peered up at the other man. 'You're certain, then, that Stefan Taber was murdered.'

'Absolutely. Telekinetic murder.'

'Telekinesis.' Sutherland repeated. 'That's moving objects at a distance.'

'Yes.'

'The object in this instance being a ten-stone man. Someone . . . or some *thing* reached out with its mind and threw the man over four hundred yards to his death.'

'Yes.'

Sutherland asked, 'Was there anything visual associated with this killing? Apart from the sight of Taber falling, I mean.'

Brady felt uncomfortable. Despite his apparent readiness to co-operate with the policeman, he was quite determined that his search for his family should *not* be made more difficult by a police presence, and he was unwilling to impart anything that he learned until such a time as it was of no further use.

But he felt distinctly that he was on the spot, now. He needed Sutherland's continued trust, and already the man instinctively knew that he had been involved in the recent chaotic attack by Arachne at Casterigg, in Yorkshire.

Without indicating his suspicion that the attack had come from the Camden area of London, Brady said, 'There was the illusion of a dog, a bloody great big black dog. It seemed to *bite* Taber. I was terrified. That hound was *big*, like a mastiff. I've also seen something similar following me today. That's all.'

'A dog,' Sutherland repeated, and clearly the information was sinking into a response-void. 'And you have no idea from whereabouts in London the attack came . . .?'

'From the north,' Brady said. 'But I say that only because we were facing Regent's Park when it happened. So somewhere from north-west to north-east'.

'Not very useful.'

'Sorry.'

Sutherland slapped his knees and stood up. He smiled at Anita, then preceded Brady to the front door. 'For my part,' he said, 'I can't offer you anything encouraging, or anything new. Your family's photographs are in every police station from the most remote village to the busiest city, in the UK and Ireland. In Room 17,' he smiled slightly, a genuine smile, 'your case is top of the list. Anything, no matter how flimsy or tentative, that comes in relating to the Bradys . . . I'll make sure you know about it.'

'Thanks.'

'We still don't know what this group is doing, this Arachne. We don't know their purpose, or how they operate, or how they're funded. They're a blank in every way except the wreckage they leave behind. The human wreckage. So if you, for your part, hear anything . . .'

'I'll brief you fully,' Brady said. The policeman nodded acknowledgement, then turned away from the house.

'Are you sure you're doing the right thing?'

Anita was standing in the middle of the lounge. She seemed agitated.

'About what?' Brady asked as he came into the room.

'Not telling Sutherland what you know.'

Brady walked over to the table and gathered up the papers where Ellen Bancroft's message was scrawled.

'I'd tell Sutherland without hesitation,' he said. 'But.a policeman's a policeman, and that means he's part of a team. I don't want vanloads of uniformed bobbies getting between me and the remaining men who took my family.'

'You might at least tell him what you know of Arachne's purpose.'

'To what end?'

With a shrug, Anita said, 'I don't know. But it might help. They might know something, or hear something . . .'

'More likely they'll go blundering about from psychic institute to psychic institute, upsetting people, alienating people and perhaps even putting Arachne on its guard. That's the last thing I want.'

'It might make them make mistakes,' Anita suggested, but Brady shook his head. He put the papers away in the bureau, and laid out fresh sheets. Then he went over to the open windows and stood, staring out into the garden.

'It might have the opposite effect,' he said. 'They make enough mistakes as it is.'

'Their arrogance,' Anita murmured, remembering what Brady had told her.

'Absolutely. They think they're invulnerable and they don't cover their traces with any particular care. That's why I've kept so close to them.'

'They won't think they're invulnerable after Anerley...'

That too was true. The team of Arachne's Collectors, sent to repair the breached Shrine which they had set up a year before, had been destroyed to a man. But it was their own unborn force of evil that had destroyed them, and not Brady. Arachne had had accidents before, and it was becoming clear to Brady that these animal-masked horrors who prowled the countryside were low-level workers, Gatherers, Collectors, Builders, Murderers... they were expendable. They were rapidly replaced.

There was a higher level of Arachne, however, which was less expendable. Their cumulative name was ... Accumulators. Their function was precisely that. To accumulate, and store in their own minds, the spirits, ghosts and demonic forces of the past which Arachne was raising from the earth, and from the dead. These living storehouses of magical power would eventually gather at a place called *Magondathog*, and Arachne's final purpose would be realised.

What was that purpose? Where was Magondathog? Why were his family, Dominick, Marianna and Alison, so important to them?

Brady had no answers to these questions. He had only his growing compulsion to find his family, and avenge them for the brutal assault that they had endured.

Dan Brady stepped out into his garden, crossing the *mazon*, passing through the *zona mandragora* and experiencing the almost painful effect on his skin of standing above one of the clay and iron earth-images that were buried a foot below the ground. These defences could trap or bar the way to people with unusual mental powers. Brady himself was developing and fashioning psychic powers, in particular the ability to slip from his body and observe the world from the point of view of a (quite literally) free soul.

He had assumed that, because he had built the defences, they would not operate to block *him*. But this pain, the sensation of dizziness and pins-and-needles that he sometimes experienced in his own garden, made him wonder if he hadn't forgotten to do something vital in the building.

Anita followed him, her arms folded across her chest. Brady asked. 'Did anything happen in the box-traps?'

'Nothing.'

'And nothing more from Ellen?'

'Nothing.'

'Nothing unusual at all?'

'Not one single, solitary thing.'

Looking around him, it occurred to Brady that his garden was a miniature version of the world that Arachne were creating, a combination of neolithic earth magic, medieval alchemy and Celtic shamanism. Even so, Brady's simple psychic defences were fragmentary things, constructed from a fragmentary knowledge. And that was not Arachne at all . . .

He knew what Arachne were doing, now, even if he didn't know why.

They were raising the past, using old magic and new magic. They were summoning the forces of mind and belief from all the ages, powerful forces, each the expression of a culture's secret knowledge and hidden talent.

First there had been the Nordic spirit, still inhabiting the skull talisman that he wore around his neck. Then the gods of the North American Indians, dispatched to England in a strange Indian girl. These were the two which Brady knew about. How many hundreds more, he wondered, had been raised quietly, and were now stored and waiting . . .?

74

Each age of man, each civilisation, had tried to form a magic of its own, to understand the secret life of nature, and of time. Each magic had drawn upon its incomplete inheritance from earlier times, and had been shaped for the magician – spells for one, herbs for another, sacrifices for a third, mathematics for a fourth, computers for a fifth . . .

Brady had come to believe that Arachne were using *all* of magic. In that way they might well fill in the gaps in knowledge that had plagued the dabblers in the secret arts for so many centuries. Combine Roman, Greek and medieval sorcery with modern physics and mathematics, and though much would overlap, each would plug the 'mystery-gaps' of the others. A worldwide cookbook of magic: Celtic gods summoned by computer; the transmutation of lead into gold using neolithic symbol magic . . .

All for a goal that Arachne called the Time of Change.

And if Brady was right, and all of history's hells were loosed upon the world, the expression Time of Change seemed far too soft. As far as humankind was concerned, if Arachne won the day then only one expression seemed appropriate:

Total eclipse.

Back in the house, Brady dissected two copies of the London *A to Z* street map, trimmed the sheets, and sellotaped them together to form a single map of North London on a scale of two and a half inches to the mile. Orientating himself by the underground station at Mornington Crescent, he drew a line that approximated to a link between the British Telecom Tower and the source of the dark cloud that had snatched Taber to his death. He drew lines to either side, to compensate for inaccuracies, and saw, rather gloomily, the way that they opened out rapidly, to encompass a fairly vast area of streets, railways, reservoirs and parkland by the time they had passed Highgate.

The attack had not come from as close as Camden Town. Finchley, Kentish Town, Highgate and Hampstead were possibilities. The origin of the attack might have come from even further north . . .

'What are you going to do?' Anita asked him as she watched him studying the road map.

'Drive around tomorrow,' he said. 'I'll start here . . .' He prodded Camden Town. 'And work my way north. I might see something, or sense something. I'll try and call it out . . .'

'What?'

'The dog.'

'It'll kill you.'

Brady fingered the amulet at his neck. The skull, with its grotesquely parted mouth, seemed to be laughing at the girl. 'With Erik the Rampant on my side I think I can give as good as I get.'

Anita stared at the trophy of Brady's first encounter with Arachne. She had never disguised her feeling that Brady was over-using the talisman. She felt uncomfortable with it, and always insisted that he remove it at night.

For his part, Brady appeared to dismiss Anita's concern; but deep down her words of warning had had an effect on him. *It'll want something back from you soon, if you're not careful.*

'Do you think she's there?' Anita asked. 'Alison, I mean.'

For a moment Brady didn't reply. He stared at the map, and the magnitude of the task, and the wildness of this shot came back to him in surges of sickening insecurity. She *had* to be there. He *had* to find her. But his conviction was based in part on the cruel taunting of Arachne, a few weeks before; and in greater part on the brief sensation of her presence in the brick jungle of North London, as detected by an edgy post-adolescent whose powers were very uncontrolled.

And yet . . . that dog! It had been called to him in response to his mental probing!

'I'm sure she's somewhere here,' he said, circling the

Highgate region with his finger. 'The spectral dog is guarding her.'

'A powerful guardian,' Anita said.

'Yes,' Brady agreed. 'She must be very important to them.'

'This looks like being the most dangerous confrontation yet . . .'

Brady straightened up and stared at the girl. Her words echoed hauntingly, and he felt himself shiver with cold apprehension. Reaching up, he unslung the Norse talisman from round his neck and placed it carefully on the table.

'Come on,' he said suddenly. 'Close and lock the windows and grab a coat.'

Anita was taken by surprise. She did as he had said, and when she came back into the room he was just putting down the phone.

'Where're we going?'

'To see a very talented lady.'

'Not another medium?'

'My life is cursed with them. But Angela Huxley is something special. She can see clearly the place that Ellen can only glimpse. Come on.'

He locked the door to the house, and Anita closed the wrought-iron gates behind them. The Land-Rover tilted violently as Brady spun it to the left, then it screeched off down the country road, towards the woman who could see the spectral life that inhabited the realm of the dead . . .

As Brady drove into the small car-space at the front of the ornately decorated country bungalow, the front door opened and Angela Huxley stepped out into the late afternoon to greet them.

She was a tall, handsome woman in her early forties. Her hair was a rich black, although shot through, now, with brilliant strands of silver. She wore a simple and very elegant blue dress and, around her neck, a thin gold chain with a pale red jewel.

'How nice to see you again, Mr Brady,' she said, as

Brady and Anita approached. She extended her hand to each of them, and her touch was cool and gentle. Brady introduced the women to each other, and then followed Angela into her crowded but exquisitely furnished sitting-room.

All around the walls there were small dark-framed pictures. The carpet was of Persian design, and intricately patterned. The chairs were deep and comfortable. On shelves, in the recesses of the room, jade and ivory statuettes of birds, animals and human forms watched the visitors through wide, perceptive eyes.

Angela's first questions were of a concerned nature: how was he faring, had he come close to his family, was he still hopeful of finding them . . . Brady talked quietly with the older woman. He seemed to Anita, watching from the deepest of the armchairs, to take great reassurance from the medium. They drank tea and ate dry biscuits. A small brass-fronted clock ticked gently, and chimed softly when it struck an evening hour.

When they had finished their tea, Angela sat back in her armchair and fixed Brady with a penetrating, quizzical stare.

'So . . .' she said softly.

'So . . .' Brady repeated, and smiled.

'You want me to look for something. Something in the Hinterland.'

'Yes.'

'What's the Hinterland?' Anita asked from across the room. Without appearing at all disturbed by the girl's intrusion, Angela briefly and pleasantly explained that the Hinterland was a part – a nearby part – of what people more generally called the 'Astral Plane'. It was the spirit realm where the consciousness of a recently dead human migrated on its way to the afterlife proper. Different spirit mediums were in tune with different parts of that Otherworld. Angela communed with the breezy, bright and occasionally mysterious level which seemed to mark the first step onwards. She called it the Hinterland. It was at times a shadowy place, at times misty. But always bright, and with a sense of the sea-shore about it. When a spirit passed beyond the sea-shore, it was lost to her.

When the explanation was finished, Brady said, 'Sometime in the early summer there was a great disturbance in the Hinterland. Am I right?'

Angela's face darkened slightly. She nodded. 'Yes. Violence and pain, a sustained scream of agony. Not one voice, but many. Over several days. I couldn't bear to listen. The voices were old.' She fiddled with a strand of her hair, watching Brady closely. 'Could you have prevented it?'

Brady shook his head. 'I came very close to Marianna. I killed one of the beasts that attacked us that night. But Arachne were very powerful in the town, and I couldn't stop the evil that they'd unleashed.'

The medium seemed satisfied, and her face brightened. 'I hope never to experience such a sound again,' she said. 'But there is something unpleasant in the Hinterland at the moment, something very sad . . .'

'I'd be glad to know what it is,' Brady said, leaning forward.

'Something has happened?' Angela asked. Brady nodded. The woman persisted, 'Something that you think will show in the Hinterland?'

'Hard to tell. I'll explain in a moment. But please: tell me of anything unusual that you are witnessing.'

Angela closed her eyes and touched her fingers lightly to the sides of her head. 'It's still there,' she whispered. 'A child . . . two children. They are very lost. One has been there for a few days. The other . . . just today. A few hours. Terrible pain, terrible anguish. Something has killed them; they are so young, nowhere near ready for the journey they must take. They'll be in the Hinterland for a long time . . .'

As she spoke, tears coursed down her cheeks, a physical reaction to the terrible emotional contact she was making with the spirits of two dead children.

Brady looked slightly impatient, although he controlled his inclination to break in and urge her to look elsewhere. The deaths of two children didn't mean anything to him.

She was silent for a while. If Taber's arrival in the Hinterland had occurred yet, she didn't mention it, or perhaps hadn't noticed it. Brady had talked to Angela before about the scope and extent of her talent, and he knew that she quite often could register violent arrivals in the Otherworld, but that she didn't necessarily see *everything* that died violently, and could not respond at all to mass death, such as occurred in a war.

There were stranger things in the Hinterland, though: fossilised spirits; wanderers; spirits passing the wrong way through the Otherworld, although for what purpose she didn't know; and shadow-shapes whose identity perplexed her, and contact with which could almost physically hurt her.

She monitored the Hinterland with great care, and great caution.

Soon the silence disturbed Brady and he whispered, 'Can you see anything to do with . . . the moon?'

Angela's eyes opened slightly, and tears that had collected inside the lids dribbled down her cheeks. But she was no longer weeping. She frowned slightly, then shook her head.

'There is something . . .' she began, without emphasis. 'Something . . . an animal . . . a large animal. In the Hinterland. An animal.'

'What sort of animal?' Brady whispered. Anita had sat bolt upright in her chair, watching with more interest.

'A dog,' Angela murmured, and Brady exchanged a quick, alarmed glance with the younger girl. The medium went on, 'A black dog. It's huge. It's running in the shadows, by the rocks. I can only just see it. The mist is thick. The dog is black. I can see its shape distantly. Now it's stopped . . . it's looking at me . . .'

Angela was frowning as she spoke, and her face had become quite white. Her hands clutched at the sides of the chair, and a sheen of cold sweat formed above her lips.

It occurred to Brady, suddenly, that the woman was in danger. Of course! If she was aware of Alison, perhaps she was somehow contacting Alison as she scanned the

Hinterland. And in so doing she had called the guardian
. . . the dog that guarded!

'Angela!' he shouted.

'The dog . . . it's coming . . .' the woman said, and her
voice began to rise to a pitch of hysterical concern.

'Stop it!' Brady yelled. He ran to her and slapped her
hard in the face. Her eyes sprang open, her mouth opened,
and a deep, full-blooded howling escaped from her lips.
The howling of a dog. It filled the room; it made Anita
cringe with fear, hiding herself behind her arms and legs,
watching through wide, scared eyes.

As suddenly as the terrifying baying had sounded, it
faded, and Angela Huxley sat trembling and shaken,
staring up at Brady through wide, slightly misted eyes.

'A dog . . .' she repeated. 'It ran at me. An awful-looking
thing.'

'I didn't expect that,' Brady said. 'I should have been
more careful. A dog killed someone earlier today. A dog
has been following me, I'm sure of it. I don't know what it
means, except . . . I think the animal is somehow guarding
Alison. Did you get any sense of a woman? Did you sense
Alison?'

Angela shook her head slowly, but frowned as she did so.
'Not Alison, no . . .'

'You don't sound sure.'

'I am sure,' Angela said. Still she seemed perplexed. 'It
was a woman . . . or perhaps three women . . . I have a
sense of three. She – they – were behind the dog, in the
mist . . . It's so confusing!' She shook her head violently,
as if trying to clear her thoughts.

Brady said nothing. He crouched by her and held her
hand, staring at the lines on the woman's face, watching as
she struggled to make sense of an image she had partly
glimpsed.

'An old woman. A very old woman. And a younger one,
like a child. Innocent . . .'

'Marianna . . .' Brady breathed quietly, but the medium
shook her head.

'Not Marianna. Older than your daugher. But innocent.

81

Youthful. And there was a third one, a third woman. Beautiful. Disturbing . . . very disturbing . . .'

'In what way?'

Angela smiled thinly and flushed. She glanced at Brady, and he detected a strange embarrassment in her. She said. 'I don't know quite what to say . . .'

'Say it anyway. It might be important.'

'Oh well,' she murmured with a sigh, then took a deep breath and closed her eyes. 'Very sexual. Very powerful in that way. For an instant as I glimpsed her I experienced a . . . a thrill. Deep inside. Ecstasy . . .' Her voice had dropped to an almost inaudible murmur. 'A powerful sense of sexual pleasure. And innocence. And age. Three women. Or one . . . I'm not sure. They were so blurred, so distant, and you slapped me awake too quickly . . .'

Brady was unabashed. 'I thought your life was in danger. I still do. Thank you for what you did, but please, don't try and contact that image again.'

'No?'

'No. The dog, if it's the same thing, has already killed once. It's a spectral guardian, with very unghostly methods of worrying at a corpse.'

'Very well. I'll take your advice. My house is guarded, though; I feel quite safe here.'

Brady pressed the woman's hand, smiled and stood up. 'I know. Even so, please be cautious.'

'I will.'

'I had no idea that you'd sense the dog – I wondered if there was anything in the Hinterland connected with the moon, or the "coming of the moon".'

Angela shook her head.

'Or with this sign . . .?'

He showed her the circular pattern with its inverted V. Angela stared at the symbol.

'No. Nothing like this. I'm sorry . . .' She looked away, still very distracted. 'Just that strange woman. It didn't feel like death . . .'

'But definitely not Alison or Marianna. Something unconnected.'

Angela made an apologetic face. 'It would seem so. I'm sorry.'

'Thanks anyway. In fact, you've been more than helpful. You've added to my conviction that Alison *is* alive, and is nearby.'

'I hope you find her. I hope you find them all.'

'Thank you.'

It was dark as they came within sight of Brook's Corner. The Land-Rover's headlights picked out trees, walls and the sleek, gleaming shapes of cars parked in the drives of the large detached houses that stood back from the road, screened by their own undergrowth.

The moon was almost full. Brady stared at it as it hung low over the trees, an oddly yellow hue.

The moon is coming –

A black dog –

Three women –

And Alison, somewhere north of Camden Town, guarded . . . but alive!

Thoughts, passions, fears coursed through his mind. Anita's hand, resting gently on his thigh, was comforting, at times arousing. He liked her company. She reminded him that part of him was human, weak and sensuous.

The bright beam of the headlights cut through the darkness. It was possible to believe that the car, and its lights, were the only living things in a wasteland of pitch black. It was an eerie sensation.

The Talisman Wall of Brook's Corner loomed ahead of them.

Anita gasped. Brady felt his heart flutter with alarm.

He slowed the Land-Rover and came to a stop outside the gates, letting the full light of the headlamps shine on the wall.

White marks covered that wall now. Strange designs, sinister figures, crosses, swastikas, inverted letters and the daubed outlines of animal skulls.

'Oh my God,' Anita whispered. 'What are they?'

'Hex marks,' Brady said. 'Witch marks. Stay in the car . . .'

'You haven't got your talisman,' she reminded him as he went to leave the vehicle. *Damn*, he thought, hesitating. He had taken the amulet off, knowing that it would disturb Angela Huxley. It was still in the house, safely hidden.

'Drive the Land-Rover,' he said to Anita, opening the door and stepping out into the cold night. Anita squeezed across into the driver's seat and revved up the engine as Brady opened the iron gates to the ground. She drove slowly past him and stopped in front of the house.

Brady closed the gates and stood for a moment, staring into the darkness, listening, smelling the crisp, cold night.

Across the road, in the dense undergrowth, there was movement. Something silvery gleamed for an instant, then faded. A human figure seemed to move among the trees. A figure in flowing robes. The robes caught the moonlight and were eerily illuminated.

The glimpse faded as quickly as it had come. There was just stillness, blackness, and the unnerving sensation of being watched.

Distantly, a dog began to bark.

5

'But we *are* in danger!' Flynn protested. 'I'm *not* making it up.'

He stood defiantly just inside his room, already dressed in his pyjamas. His mother stood over him, her hands on her hips, her face a mask of tired, irritated impatience.

'I warned you,' she said. 'I'll say nothing to your father – *provided* you clear all this nonsense from the walls tomorrow morning, *and* from Pippa's room!'

'We've *got* to be defended!' Flynn said desperately. 'I'm frightened. I'm *really* frightened. We've done something . . .'

Rosamund frowned wearily, then dropped to a crouch before her son, taking him by the shoulders and shaking him gently. 'You've got nothing to be frightened about, Errol. Your daddy and me, we've protected you as much as you need. We know how to look after you . . .'

The boy couldn't hold back the tears. His mother refused to understand. His father was downstairs watching television, tired after his long day at work and the intense meeting that he and Rosamund had just attended. Flynn didn't know what to do. Should he tell his mother *everything?* It would put *her* in danger as well, and he felt protective towards her. He couldn't endanger his parents – but they *had* to believe that he and Pippa were threatened!

'We've provoked something,' he said.

Rosamund looked at him quizzically, her face showing that she believed her son to be indulging his imagination. 'What've you provoked?' she asked.

'An evil thing. Dogs. And a witch.'

'A witch? In London?' Rosamund laughed, standing up and ruffling her son's hair.

'It's true!' he insisted.

'And that's why you painted your room with all these marks?'

He nodded soberly, staring up at his mother, who shook her head in vague amusement.

'If it was true, young man, then you would be in deep trouble. All your marks are crazy,' she whispered at him, bending down. 'They're wrong. A witch would take one look and laugh.'

Flynn was shocked. He turned away from his mother, and the charcoal charm signs seemed to writhe in front of his eyes, mocking him, laughing at him.

'They can't be wrong . . .' he whispered.

'You just make sure they're washed off the walls in the morning.'

'They can't be!'

'Do you hear me, young man?'

Flynn turned to face his mother, urgency making tears form in his eyes. 'We're in danger,' he said. 'All of us. You've got to listen to me! Gerry's dead. The witch killed him.'

'Gerry? Gerry Cronin?'

Flynn nodded glumly, his lips trembling. Rosamund frowned for a moment, then looked nervous. 'I don't like what those comics are doing to you, Errol. I think we'll have a long talk soon, about reading, and imagination . . . and lying.'

She spoke softly, sounding depressed. Flynn shook, feeling cold, feeling terribly threatened. 'He *is* dead. I saw him.'

'Where?'

'In the Mutie Wasteland,' he murmured. His mind was spinning. If he told her where they'd been she might go there, and the dogs would get her too.

'Mutie Wasteland indeed!' she said, her suspicions that this was a game confirmed. 'Get to bed, young man. And don't forget what I told you!'

Flynn backed away from her. 'If these charms aren't right, then the dogs are getting Ritchie as well. Right now. I saw them as we left.'

'Ritchie Hughes is sensible. He's in bed and fast asleep. He's the most sensible of the lot of you. Maybe I'll ask his mother for a swap . . .'

She was trying to be humorous, trying to elevate her suddenly very gloomy son.

She left the room, closing the door and turning off the light. Flynn stood in the darkness and listened. She went to Pippa's room. Then she went downstairs and he heard the low grumble of adult voices.

Half an hour later his parents came up to bed, closed the door of their room and shuffled about for a few minutes before there was silence. Flynn dressed quickly. He found the paper with the charm marks and hid it in his jacket. Right or wrong, they must do *some* good.

He realised he couldn't get any help from his parents, but he wasn't prepared to endanger *their* lives. Therefore he and Pippa had to hide. They would go to the most secure hide-out of all, the place where there was food and drink, and comics to read while they hid.

Trog City.

He crept out onto the landing and eased his way into Pippa's room, shushing her quiet when she murmured with alarm.

'Get dressed,' he whispered. 'Get your anorak and bring a blanket.'

'Where are we going?'

'Trog City.'

'Why? Aren't we safe?'

'Not any more. Come on. Mum and Dad are safe enough, but we've got to lie low.'

The girl scrambled out of bed and pulled on her jeans and jumper over her pyjamas. Flynn switched on her small desk light and wrote a short note. It read simply:

Dear Mum and Dad. We're both ever so sorry. When we were playing we provoked a hag, who has four dogs. The dogs chewed up Gerry and Tip, and are chewing up Ritchie right now. I thought the charms from your book were right. But we know a place to hide where nobody will get us. Don't worry about us. But please find the charms for a witch and dogs, because she will be looking for us. We have plenty of food and toilet paper, and lots of comics. Love Flynn and Pippa.

As an afterthought he crossed out 'comics' and wrote 'books'.

That done, they eased open Pippa's bedroom window and peered anxiously into the black night. There was no hint of silver, although the moon was high and almost full. Flynn stared at it and felt very frightened.

Then he squeezed through the window and onto the flat roof of the kitchen extension. He helped Pippa down. From the roof they shinned down a drainpipe to the back alley.

Then, with an anxious glance around them, they were off, running quietly through the streets, keeping to the absolute darkness of doorways and walls, ever watchful for that tell-tale gleam of silver moonglow.

PART TWO

6

Brady's comment to Anita, that his life was 'cursed by mediums', would have amused Françoise Jeury if she had heard it. She would have said to Brady, 'I know what you mean *exactly*!' Her own life was similarly cursed. Not a week – and sometimes not even a day – went by without her life being in one way or another affected by a person of 'talent' or an object of bizarre power.

The strange thing was: Françoise Jeury was *herself* talented. And yet she had managed to live for most of her forty-four years without the confusing and self-centred company of other psychics. She was French; she was a small, very handsome woman, with auburn hair and exquisitely Gallic features. She had lived happily in Brittany with her husband Antoine, and when Antoine's work had taken him to the Middle East, she had gone, and when her own work had taken her to Paris, she had spent the months there existing perfectly normally.

Her talent gave her problems, certainly. But it had not attracted other talented people. Now, like flies to jam, they gathered around her.

Antoine had died. She had come to England two years ago at the invitation of the man who now lay sleeping heavily beside her. And in those two years, working at the Ennean Institute for Paranormal Research, her life, like Dan Brady's had been 'cursed by mediums'.

In the early hours of a morning that would later be horrifically marked by the death of a child in the Highgate area of London, and of a young talented man called Stefan Taber, she lay thinking of Brady and staring at the dark hair on the shoulders and back of her friend, Liam Kline. He breathed loudly, his head turned away from her, his body not reacting as she gently stroked his skin.

She had woken with Brady on her mind. It disturbed her. She had seen him briefly a few months ago, and the meeting had been harrowing for her. But she was so busy these days that no single mind-encounter meant that much to her, and her sad, violent 'remembering' of Marianna had soon become just another experience. The presence of Brady's daughter had been induced through the girl's broken spectacles. Most of the memory-echo in the metal frames and glass had been of cold and fear, the girl's last emotion before the spectacles were taken from her and crushed. It had distressed Françoise to experience those emotions – during the application of her talent – and it hadn't seemed to do Dan Brady much good.

So why think of him now?

Presumably (she rationalised to herself) because of the call from Andrew Haddingham inviting her to come and look at a statuette. Another routine piece of psychic archaeology, but of course Haddingham was Brady's friend. The unconscious connection had made her dream of Brady. That was all there was to it.

Lee Kline snoozed on. Françoise felt irritated with him. She twisted round in bed and placed her feet against the small of his back. Each time she pressed down, Lee shuffled a few inches towards the edge of the bed.

After a few moments he teetered over the cliff. One final nudge with her feet and he vanished from sight, yelling loudly as he awoke with a rude start. He peered grumpily, blearily and groggily back over the side of the bed where Françoise was still laughing.

'What the hell was that for?' he muttered thickly, slowly standing up.

'It's your turn to make the coffee.'

'Oh eez eet?' he said sourly, mimicking her accent.

'Yes eet eez!' she said, mimicking the mimic. 'Hurry up. I have to get to work.' She lay back, arms above her head, and smiled, stretching slightly and yawning.

Lee stood staring at her, scratching his unshaven chin and still trying to wake up properly.

'It's Saturday,' he said grumpily. 'Day off.'

'For you maybe. Not for me. No peace for me. And no coffee either, yet. What's the matter, you forget how to make it?'

He smiled and shook his head, stepping closer to the bed. 'How do you want it?'

She closed her eyes and wriggled further down beneath the covers. 'Black and strong, please.'

'Right!' he yelled, and with one swift motion stripped the covers from the bed and flung his full, fourteen stone upon the screeching woman. Her cry of 'Brute! Animal! Sadist!' became an incoherent murmur.

She was half an hour late for her meeting with Hadding-ham, but he didn't seem to mind. He wouldn't even allow her to apologise. He seemed far more concerned that he had asked her to come out at a weekend, and seemed very relieved when she reassured him that she was quite happy to oblige at any time.

Andrew Haddingham was middle-aged, meticulously dressed and very English. He held doors open for her, made polite conversation as they walked through the corridors of the British Museum, and in general behaved in a very deferential way towards her.

This irritated her a lot, and yet she had come to expect it in England. Everyone over thirty still adopted social roles; it was implicitly assumed that unless a door was opened for her, a woman would crash straight through it, and that latrine waste was still flung from upstairs windows, making it imperative that a woman should walk on the inside.

Peculiar; old-fashioned; but tolerable. And Hadding-ham was a very pleasant and very supportive man. When he stopped apologising.

'It's a statuette,' he said, as they walked along. 'A fragment, really. Dug up out of the old river silt about a week ago. I shan't tell you any more for the moment . . .' He looked at Françoise. 'That *is* what you want, isn't it?'

93

'That's fine,' she said. 'Unbiased impressions are always important. There is one thing, however . . .'

Haddingham led the way up a narrow flight of stairs, and towards a small, bright room. 'Which is?'

'Is it dangerous? Have there been unpleasant experiences with it?'

Haddingham shook his head, ushering her into the office. 'No. Nothing dangerous. But two people who have handled the object have been very disturbed by it. Hence our interest in you.'

Françoise stepped into the office and faced the man who rose to his feet from behind the wide, cluttered desk. He was an odd-looking man, tall, very angular, with a large hooked nose, receding yellow hair and deep, alarmingly bright grey eyes. He was both very ugly and very impressive. His tweed suit hung limply on his bones. His handshake was flimsy and uncertain, and he waved his hands nervously as he spoke. He seemed terribly on edge; or perhaps just very awkward in general.

'Doctor Bertram Soames,' Haddingham announced. 'Ms Françoise Jeury.'

'Heard a lot about you, Ms Jeury,' Soames said uncomfortably. He fidgeted for a moment, hands clasped together as if in prayer.

'That's flattering,' Françoise said, and added, with her fingers crossed. 'I've heard good things about you too, Doctor Soames.'

Soames seemed surprised, and awkwardly pleased. 'Well,' he said quickly. 'How nice. Um . . . yes. Very good. Your talent is . . . um . . .' He turned back to his desk, as if to hide his embarrassment. Françoise glanced at Andrew, who smiled and winked at her.

'Startling,' Soames finished, and sat down in his chair again, clasping his hands in front of him and staring somewhere between Françoise's chin and a distant point in the room. 'Yes. Startling.'

'It's quite routine really,' Françoise said.

Soames looked up, almost meeting her eyes. 'Is it!'

'As routine as ultrasonic scanning, or carbon dating.

94

It's *all* magic to people who don't understand the laws of nature.'

Soames frowned and thought very hard for a minute, his bright grey eyes filled with an astonishing expression of incomprehension. It had never occurred to him that some psychic talent might have a sound basis in physico-chemical law.

'Psychic archaeology,' he said, and laughed nervously. 'I never thought I'd live to see the day when . . .' He trailed off, shuffled in his chair, then reached for a folder of drawings.

'When the quacks took over?' Françoise finished for him. Soamed blushed brightly, and made strenuous attempts to correct the mistaken impression. 'Oh not at all, not at all. I merely meant . . . um . . .' Looking down at the folder, he turned the papers round towards her suddenly. 'These are sketches of the fragment. Did them myself. Hawkins is still confident that the other pieces are to be found.'

Françoise didn't reach for the pages of meticulous drawings. After a moment Soames looked up again, frowning. Françoise said pleasantly, 'I can't work my magic from drawings.'

'Beg pardon?'

'Drawings,' Françoise said. 'No vibrations. No memory. No good. I need the real thing.'

Reacting as if stung by a bee, Soames snapped closed the folder with a second vocalised apology. 'Of course. How foolish of me. It's in the safe . . .'

He left the room for a minute or so and Françoise and Haddingham exchanged a smile at his expense. 'He doesn't know what to make of you,' Andrew said.

'Understatement of the year.'

With hands in his pockets, Haddingham sat on the edge of the desk and stared at the woman. 'Psychic archaeology is still in its infancy. It's like acupuncture and western medicine. It's taken years for the mysticism of the East to impress itself on the technology of the West.'

'I know. And it will take years for the paranormal to be

taken seriously here. Except that the Government is already taking it seriously.'

Haddingham nodded thoughtfully. 'Our Government isn't prepared to miss a trick. It has the money to play several hands. Donations and bequests from people like Koestler have helped.'

'Hillingvale is a big place,' Françoise said. 'That takes a lot of funding. And it's a big interest in psychic research by your government.'

'The Ennean, where you are, is bigger. A little less controlled, but bigger. A lot of work at Hillingvale is for the Ministry of Defence. Well, it's all for the MoD of course, but a lot is specifically designed to be of use in wartime situations. Psychic warning. Premonition. Psychic eavesdropping . . .'

'How horrible,' Françoise said, walking round the small museum office.

'But very British,' Haddingham pointed out.

'That's true,' murmured Françoise soberly. 'It will be the same in France soon. And it must be the same in America. Right-wing governments exercising right-wing interests. Playing with war toys.' She stared at Andrew Haddingham for a long moment. The man didn't flinch under her gaze, but cocked his head in silent enquiry.

'Why are you interested in this statuette?' she asked suddenly.

'That's easy,' he said. 'Anything like a statue, or a weapon, that comes out of the ground at an excavation, gets a routine scan at Hillingvale. We have electronic equipment there that *can* detect residual energy, or recorded noise, in a crystal structure . . . like stone, or pattern-forged metal . . .'

'Pattern-forged rust, you mean.'

'It's a crude technique, certainly,' Haddingham said with a shrug. 'We also have talented people who can get *ideas* about objects, and indicate any that might be of interest –'

'Paranormally, not historically.'

'Well, yes. This particular statuette came out yesterday

for the routine scan, in a crate of stuff from the Walbrook Excavations. It had to come back to the BM, but it had already registered something rather unusual. A regular, rhythmic pulse of energy. Like a heartbeat . . .'

'You shouldn't tell me this. If I was a quack, I could use it.'

'But you're not a quack,' Haddingham said with a thin smile. 'And I trust you.' He stood up from the desk as Soames came back into the room. 'It's the oddest thing *I've* experienced in an archaeological fragment like this.'

'A heartbeat,' Françoise murmured, watching as Soames placed a small crate on his desk. And as she spoke she couldn't control the shudder that suddenly coursed through the body.

'This is all the artefact material from the site so far,' Doctor Soames said, as he took out the linen-wrapped objects and placed them on the desk. Each package was labelled. They had been very carefully kept. One object was a flat piece of marble, which Soames unwrapped and stared at for a second before turning to Haddingham.

'Did you see this?'

Haddingham nodded, but took the marble slab and turned it towards Françoise. Deeply inscribed on the marble, as if scratched rather than created by any craftsman, were the words IC HABIT LUN.

'*Hic habitat luna,*' Soames said. 'The fragment is broken, and the words are probably provincial slang.'

'*Here lives the moon,*' Françoise translated, and reached out to touch the inscription. She felt a tingle of unease, but nothing more powerful.

'Indeed,' Soames said. '*Here lives the moon.* A temple to the moon, I believe. The whole site being excavated was probably part of the shrine.' He took the marble inscription back and stared at it. 'This was probably some sort of votive plaque. It's too crude to have been official. A graffito probably. A sort of prayer offering . . .'

Here lives the moon . . .

The words were a disturbing and haunting echo to Françoise. She could hardly hear Soames as he prattled on. She stared at the angrily scratched words – angrily? Why did she think they were angry? She could feel the pain in them, the haste, the desperation. There was fire in them. Fire. Where did that come from? IC HABIT LUN. The spidery letters wriggled on the green marble. She reached out and gently touched the slab once more.

She ducked as the sword struck towards her. She could hear its ringing sound, as it impacted with stone, or marble.

IC HABIT LUN.

HIC HABITAT LUNA . . .

Running. Fear. Fire.

'. . . a Roman temple to the Moon Goddess,' Soames was saying.

'Not Roman,' Françoise said quickly, and the two men looked at her sharply.

'Not Roman?' Soames said.

'It's a warning. *Here lives the moon.* It's a warning . . .'

'A warning . . .' Soames repeated, still staring down at the inscription. 'Well, well. A warning. But I don't think so, somehow. Although the statue is unusual for a Roman carving. Probably British, and taken over by the provincial settlers . . .'

'Doctor Soames!' Françoise said, and her voice was more than tinged with irritation. Soames glanced at her edgily. He said nothing, frowning, looking uncomfortable. 'Doctor Soames,' the woman said again, less sharply. 'I apologise. But I must have certain conditions to work in. I find you very distracting. Please don't think me rude, but I can only work in a supportive atmosphere. I know that you find it hard to grasp psychic archaeology, to understand what I'm doing, or how. I can't explain it. I just do it. But I would be very grateful if you would leave me and Doctor Haddingham alone for a few minutes.'

Soames straightened up, looking at Haddingham, then at the small wooden crate. He reached into the crate and brought out a bulky, wrapped object, the size of a wine bottle. This he placed on the desk, acting slowly, deliberately, as if trying to make up his mind what he should do.

'Very well,' he said huffily. 'I shall be on extension 44. Ring through when I'm to be allowed back.'

'I'm sorry,' Françoise said, as he walked stiffly past her.

'Don't be. I quite understand,' Soames lied.

When he had gone, Françoise felt her whole body relax. She even sighed her relief, grinning at Haddingham. 'Unbelievers,' she said. 'Unbelievably distracting.'

'I can understand,' Haddingham agreed. 'I've seen it happen too often, this collapse of the infra-aura, not to agree with you.'

'Why does it always happen?' Françoise asked, as she walked to the desk and stared down at the linen-wrapped artefact labelled 'Statue 3HWal'.

Haddingham shrugged. 'From what we know of the infra-aura –'

'I hate that description. It's meaningless.'

'*Electro-magnetic resonance at a distance* is too cumbersome. *Coincidental EM power reflectivity and refractive vibration* is too . . . incomprehensible. We use *infra-aura* because we can detect the emanation from a psychic, and before it forms radial low-energy cables, or psychic strands as some people call them, the expression is like a series of images of the person within.'

'With image-decay becoming pronounced, I know. Some sort of primitive nightmare expression at the very outside. I wonder what mine looks like.' She smiled, touching the wooden crate with one long, thin finger. 'I find it hard to imagine that as I walk about there are several increasingly ugly images of me walking as well.'

'*I* find it odd that those images have only been detected by real-space, real-time technological equipment, and not by other psychic means. It's as you just said, Françoise. It's all magic to people who don't understand science. It's all science when the rules and laws are understood.'

'Except that in science, the scepticism of the experimenter can't affect the performance. With me, a hostile aura can break my own.'

'We're working on how that happens at Hillingvale,' Haddingham said. 'When we get an answer, and can demonstrate it, a lot of psychic-debunkers are going to have to eat their words.'

'A lot of debunked psychics are going to help them,' Françoise pointed out.

'True. Anyway. Let's have a look at 3HWal, shall we?'

Even before he had fully unwrapped the statue, Françoise had been affected by it. She stood watching Haddingham as he peeled the linen wrapping from the object, and she found that she couldn't move, or speak, or think of anything other than the sensation in her mind. Part of her wanted to run. Part of her argued, quite rationally, that the only violence a violent memory could do was in inducing a violent action – the memory itself, no matter how disgusting or distressing, could not harm her.

But a smell filled her nostrils – a psychic smell. She had experienced it before. Often. It was the smell she associated with meat that had been left too long in a warm place, a sharply unpleasant smell. The smell of blood.

She was too old, too experienced, too hardened to gag. But she disliked sensing blood. It made her feel dull, made her edgy. It ruined her appetite. The smell almost always prefaced a mental video nasty, and she could well do without such 'historical' recollections.

'What a beauty,' Haddingham said, but became solemn as he saw the expression on Françoise's face. 'Are you all right?'

'I feel sick,' she said, not taking her eyes from the *thing* that he held.

It was the statue of a woman. That was evident from the breasts that had been sculpted. The stone figure was naked. The pubic area was eroded, but still clearly indicative of a large pudendal swell and vulval entry. The figure's head was missing, although the shoulders of the image could still be seen to be covered with long hair.

From the belly of the figure a child's face stared blindly, innocently into space. Curled hair around the smooth features suggested that it was female. The mouth seemed to smile and was slightly open. The eyes were the strangely sightless eyes associated with Celtic images of severed heads.

Below the belly and the swollen pudendum, one of the legs was missing. The other was intact. The thigh was human. Below the knee, the leg was the calf, fetlock and hoof of a horse.

The whole statue was dull grey in colour. Its surface was pitted and weatherworn, but not in the same way as the lichen-covered standing stones of the West Country. The marks were more like water damage and the scratching of stones.

'Oh my God,' Françoise said quietly. Haddingham was staring at her in something approaching astonishment.

'Has it affected you already?'

She nodded. 'It's awful. It's so ugly.'

Haddingham looked down. 'It's the most unusual thing I've seen. Like yet unlike Iron Age stone carving. I find it – compelling. Very beautiful. It fills me with awe. It frightens me.'

'It frightens me, too,' Françoise said with a quick, nervous laugh. 'I don't know . . . I've had bad experiences too many times not to be warned by my instincts. I smell blood . . .'

'Can you sense the heartbeat?'

She shook her head. 'Not that, no. Where did it come from?'

'An excavation in the City. London, I mean. What they call an "opportunity excavation".'

Françoise shrugged, not understanding.

'A fire, I think,' Haddingham explained. 'In the cellars of a fairly old building. It stands on the banks of what was once the most important river to London . . .'

'The Walbrook?' Françoise said.

'That's right. It used to flow where the heart of the City now stands. Most of Roman London is below that particular concrete jungle, so the British Museum takes every opportunity to snoop around in the dirt. This fire meant that a building was demolished, and will be rebuilt. The museum has a few months to dig up and record whatever it can. The foundations hadn't destroyed the deep layers, and out of the old river silt came' – he hefted the statue in his hands – 'came this little beauty. Probably from a temple.'

'This thing isn't Roman,' Françoise said, her voice almost a whisper.

'No it isn't. But the early city was a mixture of natives, colonials and merchants. There must have been temples to local deities, as well as to the Roman ones . . .'

'It's evil,' she said, shaking her head, afraid to touch the statue. 'I'm sorry. I'm almost frightened to let it have contact with me.'

Andrew Haddingham was nothing if not a perfect gentleman. He looked disappointed, but picked up the linen wrap and began to cover the statue. 'My dear Ms Jeury, I wouldn't dream of asking you to risk your sanity, or whatever. I'm most grateful for you coming out. I'm disappointed, of course, but I'm too well acquainted with the nature of the supernatural these days to dismiss what you say lightly.'

'Thank you,' Françoise said. 'But I haven't said that I *won't* try and divine whatever is recorded in the object. I'm just frightened. I think I should take certain precautions.'

After watching her for a moment, Haddingham quickly uncovered the statue again and placed it on the desk. He stared at it, touching it gently. 'There is a heartbeat within it. It is a haunted thing, we're quite certain of that. It seems to be associated with a glow, a moonglow. You know, silvery white light. Two people have sensed such a thing in the few days that the statue has been in the museum. But it's the heartbeat that intrigues us.' He looked up and smiled self-consciously. 'I shouldn't really refer to it as such, of course. The energy output merely reflects the sort of heartbeat pattern you can see on an oscilloscope . . .'

'OK . . .' Françoise said, and took a deep breath. She removed her coat, rolled up her sleeves, and then checked the window. It was locked, and the glass was thick. There

102

was a three-storey drop to the concrete courtyard below.

She walked around the room quickly, opening drawers, and searching on top of the filing cabinet and on the various shelves. She found a stainless steel paper-knife and gave it to Haddingham.

'Do you know how to administer oral resuscitation?' she asked.

'The kiss of life? Certainly.'

'Good.' She quickly rolled up a copy of the London *Evening Standard* to make a tight tube of paper. 'For my teeth,' she said, passing this too to Haddingham. 'You know, if I seem to be having an epileptic fit. Get it between my jaws fast. I like my tongue.'

Haddingham shuddered, but accepted the roll of newspaper and stood back.

'Otherwise,' Françoise said, stepping close to the statue, 'let me shriek and squirm to my heart's content. Don't be alarmed.'

She drew a deep breath into her lungs, then slowly exhaled it.

A fire burned distantly . . .

'OK,' she said. 'I'm ready.'

A cold wind, a bitter winter's day. The flame red against a dark sky . . .

She picked up the statue.

Images and memories overlap chaotically. Screaming and pain, love and silence, movement and fire, all these things tumble around inside her head, the history of the stone, a savage history, a magic one. She concentrates . . .

She is on a hill. The hill has been partly cleared of woodland to form an enclosed glade. She looks out through the break in the wall of trees, across a densely wooded lowland. In the distance, bright orange fire against a smoke-blackened sky . . . a city burns . . .

A cold wind blows the trees.

She can smell blood, there is blood on her hands, fresh spilled life. The flames of the dying city are great flickering tongues. It is not possible to hear the screams of the dying, or the ferocious crackling of wood and thatch burning, but the huge conflagration seems to suck the air from the land around. It sucks the breath from her lungs . . .

Someone – a woman – is wailing, a chanting wail, the sound of ritual.

She watches the destruction of the city in the south. In front of her stand two women, their bodies swathed in black robes, their hair long, lank, mostly grey in colour. When they turn they have the faces of wizened hags, drawn cheeks, sunken eyes, deathly grins.

Between them they hold a girl. She is dressed in white. Her face is young, her hair black. She is kneeling and her hands are tied behind her back. She kneels between stones, an altar in a place that is a shrine. On the stones are faces, the carved faces of the witchmoon, the signs of the power that controls these black-dressed women.

The witchmoon. The girl is sacrificed to this entity. Her scream is brief, her pain short-lived. They mix with the screams and pain of others, so many others, so many centuries. The smell of blood is stronger, the life-force in the stone stronger – her skull is smashed. They have used the stone to smash open her head, releasing her life to the wind.

The stone sucks up that life.

The images swirl, like water. There is the sound of water. The darkness of a cavern, the flickering of a torch, the sound of shuffling feet. This is the new place. The *new* place. They have come here from the temple. Moonglow illuminates rock walls, wet walls, the claustrophobic low space of the tunnel through which the river flows . . .

Image: a woman of mature years, dressed in a check robe, with a broad, heavy cloak around her shoulders, stands and holds the stone. Her hair is long and brilliant red, her eyes are fierce, her face scarred. Behind her, a great army of dusty, weary men in chariots, on horse or on foot, stands silently on the lowland. The air is full of the smell of ash, of burning, of death. And of sweat. The very earth sweats in the silence of the moment of worship.

Then sounding soft in the silence, but growing in volume . . .

A heartbeat.

It is a rhythmic sound, and a sinister one. It is not one heartbeat but many, many hundreds, the voices of the dead, the lives which have been sucked into the stone during the worship of the moon.

A drumbeat of agony . . .

A pulsebeat of sacrifice . . .

The music of dying . . .

Growing louder, coming closer . . .

Shrouded by fire . . .

Burning!

He had sensed, rather than known, that all was not well with Françoise. For some seconds, he had watched her, and alarm bells had begun to ring. She had been in contact with the statue for more than five minutes. During the last minute a curious change had come over her.

Her eyes were closed, but she had slumped to the floor, legs spread out, arms clutched to her chest, the statue held like a child. Her mouth gaped. Andrew dabbed at the persistent stream of saliva that trickled down her chin, but her blouse was still soaked.

She made no sound for a while.

Then her eyes opened to a wild stare, unfocused. She began to sway.

She began to murmur. A rhythmic sound. She was saying, 'Fire . . . fire . . . fire . . .' and her face became red, her body more agitated.

The scream, when it came, was expected, but still very shocking; Haddingham reached forward to break the contact between woman and statue, but hesitated.

The scream faltered.

Françoise's stare became a look of fixated panic. Haddingham desperately wanted to help her, but he remembered her words: *Let me shriek and squirm to my heart's content.*

'What do I do?' he whispered at her. 'What shall I do?'

She shuddered violently, clutching the statue more tightly. She was still making a sound, although it was now incoherent. But slowly the sound rose in volume, a gurgling noise, an expression of rising panic.

'Françoise . . . *Françoise*!'

She screamed again, and this time there was such *agony* in the cry! Her mouth stretched wide, her eyes screwing up as the pain coursed through her.

'O God!' Haddingham cried, and reached towards the statue.

A strange silvery glow began to form around her body. Andrew hesitated in his movement, fascinated, appalled. The glow grew in intensity. A manifestation of the infra-aura? He didn't know. The gleaming shroud brightened, and suddenly it began to flicker. But the flickering was like fire, and as he watched closely so he realised that it *was* fire –

Still she screamed.

Now he reacted without further confusion. He wrenched at the statue in her grasp, tried to take it from her. She held on passionately. He gasped as he touched the stone –

It was hot! It was physically hot!

'Françoise! Let go!' he yelled.

Her scream persisted. Only when he prised her fingers loose from the stone statue did she let go, but she still tried to keep it, reaching for it, her fingers curled and grasping.

The ghostly flames faded from her. Her scream subsided and her gaze became normal. He placed the hot statue on the desk and blew on his burned fingers. (There was no reddening or damage to the skin, he noticed.) Slowly Françoise came to her senses, and slowly she stood up again. Her legs were wobbly, her body shaking. Haddingham helped her to her feet, sat her down behind the desk, then fetched a glass of water from the washroom.

'Thank you,' she whispered, sipping the water, then draining it down. She took several deep, luxurious breaths, her eyes half closed. Then she asked for more water, and used it to splash her face and neck.

'That's better. My throat is sore. Did I scream?'

'Indeed you did,' Haddingham said. 'I let it happen for a while, then you started to . . .' What should he say? What *had* he seen. 'Well, burn,' he finished.

'I was burning?'

'Silvery flame. All over. And the statue was hot to touch. Very hot.'

Françoise stared into the middle distance, then at the broken, headless image before her. 'I saw a city burning. I saw a child brutally killed. I saw an underground river. I saw some sort of primitive ritual, moon goddess worship, I think. I saw a tall woman, a Celtic woman, ugly with scars, but a leader. And fire . . . always fire. This idol, this *thing* . . .' She leaned forward as she spoke, peering at the face of innocence that stared so blindly from the belly of the female figure. 'It has been drenched with blood often; and carried through fire many times. It is inhabited by the ghosts of its victims. But they are nourishment for the woman within. The female entity within.'

Andrew stepped slightly forward. He frowned at Françoise, then at the statue. 'What female entity?'

'Hard to tell,' Françoise whispered, shivering a little and sitting back, further from the silent, sinister icon. 'The moon, I think. An entity which we think of as a moon goddess. Worshipped in human form as a woman. Worshipped by women, by witches.'

Haddingham, despite his nervous apprehension of the statue, picked it up and turned it over in his fingers. 'And is the heartbeat the sound of this entity? Or of the victims?'

Françoise could only shrug her shoulders. 'I don't know. Something of both, I think.'

His hands were shaking as he held the source of this incredible power. He took a deep breath and smiled at the psychic. 'What an incredible "tool" you are, if you'll pardon the expression. You've glimpsed the history and the meaning of this object. You've hinted at a much more sinister type of moon worship than we'd known before. And Soames thinks that psychic archaeology is quackery!'

'He's entitled to his reservations,' Françoise said dully.

'Indeed. But I would like to record what you saw, what you felt, in detail. Is that all right?'

'Of course,' Françoise said easily. 'It's what I expected.'

'Come out to Hillingvale. I'll give you supper at my house. It's only an hour's drive from where you live.'

Haddingham cradled the stone in his hands, thinking hard, shaking his head as if he still couldn't quite believe what Françoise claimed to have seen, yet fascinated by the implied power in the object.

'I want to take this back to Hillingvale. Soames will have to let me. I won't brook any argument. What extension is he on, did he say?'

'Forty-four.'

Haddingham quickly wrapped the statue in its linen cover, then rang for Doctor Soames. As they waited for him to arrive, Andrew asked, 'Are you prepared to make the contact again? I would like to get the encounter on film. That ghostly fire . . . I've never seen anything like it.'

'Once more,' she agreed. 'Just once more. I don't trust this particular encounter.'

'It could be physically dangerous, you mean?'

'That's exactly what I mean. But I'll do it again. Just once.'

She stood up and pulled on her jacket, leaving the small room just as Soames entered, acknowledging him briefly. Behind her, Haddingham started to lie about what had occurred, and arranged for a second loan of the precious carving.

7

At seven in the morning the phone rang. Brady was stretched out in a deep bath, contentedly scrubbing his nails. He heard Anita fumble for the receiver. Her voice was a sleepy murmur, then she called, 'It's Superintendent Sutherland . . .'

Damn, Brady thought. What the hell did *he* want?

He eased himself from the hot bathwater, wrapped a towel around his waist and padded wetly into the bedroom. Anita had already turned away, and was buried beneath the covers.

'Don't you ever sleep?' Brady asked, as he spoke to the policeman.

'I never bank on it,' Sutherland said. His voice was hoarse. He sounded very tired. 'With luck I'll get a couple of hours as soon as I put the phone down.'

'What can I do for you?'

'Nothing,' Sutherland said wearily. 'I have something that might interest you, that's all. Might help. But you'll have to act with discretion.'

'I'm listening.'

'You said you saw the image of a black dog when Taber was killed . . .'

'Yes.'

'And you yourself saw a dog following you home. A spectral hound. Is that right?'

'Quite right.'

'OK. A boy, nine years of age, name of Aiden McGeary, was killed a few days ago. Strangled, then savaged by what's estimated as two dogs. Two dogs of abnormal size, according to the bite radius . . .'

Brady was instantly alert, instantly interested. 'Was this witnessed?'

'No. Pathologist's evidence is all.'

'I didn't read about it . . .'

Sutherland laughed. 'You won't, either. Can you imagine the effect if this got out? Man-and-dog killer team in North London . . .'

North London!

'. . . there would be mayhem. No dog-owner would be safe. No man and his dog would be safe. No *dog* would be safe. No, sir. You won't be reading about *this* in the paper, which is why I say I want you to act with discretion. There's more. I'd not really noticed the McGeary boy's killing. But last night there was a second murder . . . although murder is an odd word. This kid, Richard Hughes – I'll give you the address in a minute – was savaged by dogs which somehow got into his bedroom. No strangulation. His parents heard him screaming. The father *saw* what looked like a dog running away through the garden . . .'

'How big?'

'The garden?'

'The dog.'

'Big. He said the size of a horse, but that's not possible. Is it?'

'God knows,' Brady said, and remembered the size of the image he'd seen, when standing half way up the British Telecom Tower. 'Why have you decided to tell me this?'

Sutherland laughed sourly at the end of the line. 'Because it makes no sense to us, but maybe it'll make some sense to you. And if it does, I'll expect to be the first copper that you inform. I hope that's understood.'

'Fully,' Brady said, and added, 'You say this happened in North London?'

Sutherland gave him the address of the Hughes family. 'I've notified the local force that you're coming in. They're keeping a low profile at the moment. And the parents are – I hardly need to say this – in a very distressed state. Handle them gently. The McGeary parents are more approachable at the moment, obviously.'

'Thank you for your trust,' Brady said. He shivered

with chill, and tugged the towel tighter round his waist.

'Necessity is a brother to trust,' Sutherland said poetically, and Brady laughed. The policeman added, 'Besides, you seem to be able to worm things out of people that a simple copper like me can't get at.'

'I'm playing you straight,' Brady said.

'I'm sure you think you are,' Sutherland retorted. He hesitated for a second, and Brady caught that moment's pause. He waited. Then the policeman said, 'Dogs. Black dogs.'

'What about them?'

'You're searching for your wife, and a black dog attacks you. Two kids get killed by dogs. A connection seems obvious. But your wife is held by Arachne . . . dogs and Arachne. Is there a link? Are we up against Arachne again?'

Brady was almost certain that that was the case. How could there be any doubt? But until he knew *exactly* what Alison's circumstances of imprisonment were, he decided that it would be wise to play down his certainty.

'I hope so,' he said. 'But I don't know. Perhaps by this evening I shall. I'll call you.'

'Do that.'

The house where the Hughes boy had been killed was about half a mile outside the narrow band of London which Brady had drawn to encompass the source of Taber's attacker. The area was very crowded, very run down. The houses were in terraces, plain-fronted and badly decorated. Cars lined the streets, many of them just wrecks being salvaged or gradually repaired.

This part of London was quite high up, the streets sloping gradually towards Parliament Hill, Highgate Hill and the other high ground that surrounded the clay basin of the city. He could see the British Telecom Tower, a distant grey shape, apparently much further away than it really was.

He also noticed the fairly heavy police presence in the

area. Too many white Rovers, too many pale blue Panda cars, slowly driving through the narrow streets, to be routine. At the Hughes house, two plain-clothes men were talking in the street outside, and two younger policemen, in jeans and leather jackets, were having a quiet, discreet word with a neighbour. There were no flashing blue lights, no overt signs that anything was wrong.

Brady parked his Land-Rover and walked to the house. He made himself known, and was taken through the house to the back garden, where two men were crouched by the fence at the bottom, prodding at the soil. One of these was Inspector Ray Logan, a man of about Brady's age, hard-faced, fair-haired, an obvious East Ender. He seemed very irritated that Brady was there and that he had to bother with him. He came over and nodded curtly, looking Brady up and down before saying coldly, 'I'm told you might be helpful.'

'It's possible.'

'I'm told I've got to co-operate with you.'

'That's a good start.'

'You're a psychic, is that right? Close your eyes, hold your breath, and you'll see all . . .' The man's tone was sneering. Brady simply smiled and shook his head.

'There's more to it than that. What happened here?'

Logan looked round, then glanced up at the nearest bedroom window and pointed a finger. 'The kid was in bed, up there. The parents were downstairs and heard the boy start screaming. When they got to his room they found the door closed and locked from the inside. The father broke it down. The window was closed.' Logan met Brady's gaze. 'The kid was slumped below the window, torn to pieces. The father glimpsed a dog running over the fence at the bottom of the garden. A very *big* dog, he says . . .'

'But the window was closed. And the door was locked . . .'

Logan nodded. 'And there are no tracks, no prints, nothing. If the dog jumped from the window to the lawn, it would have left a mark. But nothing. And there were two

112

different animals involved, two dogs, one slightly smaller than the first.'

'Cause of death?'

'Severing of the carotid by a canine canine.'

'That's a very physical effect for a bite by a phantom dog . . .'

'Phantom dog . . .' Logan breathed wearily, and thrust his hands into his pockets as he looked around the garden.

Brady asked, 'What do we know of the boy's activities during the day?'

'He spent the morning playing with friends, the afternoon in his room. He was upset about something, his father says. Then in the evening two kids came and played with him. They left at ten. The Hughes boy got some milk, said goodnight and turned in. The next thing the parents knew, he was screaming about "dogs" and thrashing about on the floor.'

'Who were the kids who came in the evening?'

'West Indian couple, brother and sister. Wherever they went after, they and their parents aren't at home at the moment. One thing, though. All three kids were friends of a boy who was killed in the same way a few days ago . . .'

'Aiden McGeary.'

'That's right. They were all part of the same gang. They were all comic freaks; you know, horror, sci-fi, war comics. This kid's room is a shrine to the stuff. Posters, black magic, weird stuff everywhere . . .'

'Black magic,' Brady said quietly. 'Was he dabbling? Was he mucking about with magic?'

The policeman shrugged. 'I don't think so, not in any serious way. You can check the room out. I don't think it was more than a game.' Logan laughed sourly. 'Christ, the kid wasn't even ten years old.'

That doesn't mean a thing, Brady thought, as he went back into the house and quietly climbed the stairs. He could hear the sound of crying coming from behind the closed bedroom door at the end of the landing. Interspersed with the woman's grief was the soft, low murmuring of Ritchie Hughes' father. Brady felt like an

113

intruder, and it made him very uncomfortable. He hesitated for a moment, wondering whether to knock and explain what he was doing there, but he changed his mind and stepped quickly and quietly into the dead boy's room.

It was much as Logan had described it, a shrine to the world of the comic-book hero. Posters, cut-outs, collages and models cluttered the place totally. On the white carpet, by the window, was an immense blood-stain, and dark string formed the outline of the boy's body. But Brady glanced at this sombre evidence of murder only briefly. It was the signs on the walls that fascinated and surprised him.

'Good God,' he said aloud, and reached out to touch one of the charcoal-drawn symbols. It was a cross above a star, with a crudely drawn skull on the end of each cross-piece. Written in inverted letters, and formed into a circle, was the name BARON SAMEDI. On a third wall were representations of skulls, with knives drawn through them. On the fourth wall were more inverted letters, making nonsense words, and a moon symbol.

Brady felt a prickle of sweat on his face. He also felt utterly confused. He looked at the outline of the boy's body and wondered what on earth – or in hell – young Ritchie Hughes had been dabbling with. These scrawled symbols were new, violent, and inconsistent with the rest of the room.

A movement behind him made him turn, startled. The man who stood there, his eyes dark-ringed and bloodshot with crying, was in his late thirties, a stocky, chubby man, with his white shirt opened at the neck.

'You must be Ritchie's father,' Brady said.

The man nodded. 'Are you police?'

'I'm working with the police,' Brady said. 'I'm a specialist.'

'A specialist in what?' the man asked miserably. As he spoke he stared at the bloodstain, and tears welled up in his eyes.

'In this,' Brady murmured, and when he had Hughes' attention again he pointed to the walls. Hughes shook his head slowly. 'It was those other kids did that. Not Ritchie. I'm sure not Ritchie . . .'

'What are their names?'

'Flynn and Pippa Thompson. Nice kids. We look after them when their parents are out. They sometimes looked after . . .' He broke off in mid-sentence, choked up, trembling.

Brady said quickly, 'So it was the Thompsons who scrawled all this charcoal. Not Ritchie . . .'

'Ritchie was upset about something,' Hughes said, his voice little more than a whisper. 'They play all sorts of games. I'd have given Ritchie a belting for ruining the wallpaper. Just a game, I suppose.' His voice broke and tears ran freely down his face. He was crying soundlessly, looking at the walls, shaking his head. Suddenly, his voice a wailing cry, he said, 'I'd let him scribble over the whole house if he'd just come back. O God, O God . . . Ritchie . . . why? Why him? Poor Ritchie . . .'

Openly sobbing, Hughes went over to the bed and sat down heavily. Brady watched him, embarrassed and awkward. He was still intrigued by the markings on the wall. Something wasn't right . . .

'Let me ask you, Mr Hughes . . . was Ritchie frightened of something? Did he give the impression of being haunted?'

Hughes sniffed loudly, and squeezed his nose with two fingers. Then he wiped the back of his hand across his eyes, took a deep breath and straightened up, staring at Brady.

'Hard to say. They were all – all the kids – very upset by Tip's death . . .'

'The McGeary boy?'

'Yes. They were all the same gang. Called themselves Death Unit 2000. They were all sensible kids, and as far as I know they played all over the area round here. I trusted Ritchie. I trusted them all. You've got to these days, haven't you? You can't be too protective. Breeds resentment. I gave Ritchie my trust. I knew he'd behave sensibly. I knew he wouldn't invite trouble.' Hughes frowned, staring at the blood-stained carpet. 'When he

115

came back yesterday, he was upset. These marks weren't on the wall then. Flynn and Pippa came round in the evening and I could hear them mucking about up here. Maybe . . . maybe Ritchie thought that the same man who killed Tip was after him. Maybe this was a sort of barrier to evil. Flynn's father, he's – you know – a *part* of that tradition. Voodoo. Magic. It's all nonsense. Flynn was trying to help . . .'

Trying to help! Brady didn't voice the sudden thought that came to him: that perhaps this boy Flynn had *drawn* the phantom killer to Ritchie Hughes' bedroom. Perhaps deliberately, perhaps by mistake . . . but the attraction of an evil force to an evil sign was a well-known phenomenon. Flynn Thompson, with the best of intentions, may have set up his young friend like a rat in a trap.

Black dogs. Voodoo signs. North London. Alison Brady . . .

Brady stared at the sorrowful man before him, and nothing connected, nothing made sense. Except that if the dogs were guarding Alison, then maybe Ritchie Hughes had played a little too close to the place where she was being kept . . .

Or maybe Flynn Thompson, or his father, was working with Arachne. A child *could* be involved; Brady had already met a sinister and powerful young girl, albeit one who had turned *against* her one-time Masters.

An answer might be found, but it would be found with the West Indian boy. And neither he, nor his family, were at home, Logan had said.

Brady took his leave of the Hughes household, left his Land-Rover where it was and walked the streets towards the Thompsons' address. It took him ten minutes. Some of the roads were busy, and he passed through one small shopping centre which was quite crowded. Every time he saw a black youngster he wanted to stop and ask the kid's name, but he resisted the temptation.

There was an unmarked police car parked just down the road from number 72. Brady noticed two men sitting inside it, both reading tabloid newspapers. They glanced at him as he passed, then showed more interest in him as he turned into the gate and knocked on the brightly painted front door.

There was no answer. The house was in a terrace and he couldn't see round the back. He walked back to the gate and looked up and down the street, studiously ignoring the parked car and its watching occupants.

Then, at the end of the road, he saw a black couple standing watching him. As they saw that Brady had seen them, they turned and disappeared.

Trying not to advertise his haste, Brady walked back the way he had come. Once out of the policemen's view, he ran. He rounded the corner and saw the two people hurrying along the road, through the shops. The woman glanced nervously back over her shoulder.

Brady hailed them, but they ignored him. He caught up with them in a few seconds. They stopped and stared deliberately into a shop window, and feigned surprise when he spoke to them at close quarters.

'Are you Flynn Thompson's parents?' he asked.

The man looked angry. He stared hard at Brady, then glanced at the woman with him. She was several years younger than her husband, and looked more curious than frightened.

'Who are you?' she asked. 'The police?'

Brady shook his head. 'No. Not the police. There are two policemen watching your house, though.'

The man made an angry sound. To the woman he said, 'What did I tell you!'

She ignored him, still staring at Brady. 'What do you want with us? Who are you?'

'My name's Brady. Daniel Brady. I've just been talking to Ritchie Hughes' father –' The Thompsons exchanged an uneasy glance. 'Please believe what I say to you, and trust me. I'm *not* with the police. In fact, I think the police could be dangerous to us both in this situation.'

'What situation would that be?' Thompson asked.

'The killings. The black dogs. I want to talk to you quietly, and ask a question or two of your son.'

Mrs Thompson shook her head, a gesture of despair and perhaps sadness. 'For your information, mister, we'd like to ask him some questions too.'

Her husband shushed her, but she would have none of it. She stepped forward, her gaze direct and penetrating. Brady let her words circle for a moment, and then grasped what she was saying.

'He's run off?'

'Him and his sister. They vanished last night.'

'After playing with Ritchie Hughes . . .'

She nodded. Her husband looked grim. He said, 'Don't tell this man too much, Rosa.' To Brady he said, 'We don't know who the hell you are . . . What's *your* interest in our boy?'

That was a tough question to answer. Mainly because Brady had very little idea what to ask Flynn, if he found him; he was playing a long shot. He looked around, uneasy at this open street confrontation. There were too many police in the area, and it worried him.

'Was Flynn afraid of something?'

Rosa Thompson nodded. 'I thought it was a game. But they've done something, they've uncovered something . . .'

'The black dogs.'

'They're witch dogs,' she said, and her husband said loudly. 'That's *enough*! This man don't need to know those things.'

'Yes I do,' Brady said emphatically. 'That's why I've been looking for you.'

'Why?'

'A year ago my family were kidnapped,' Brady said steadily. 'Abducted. I don't know who by. I haven't seen them since. But what's got them is nothing natural. One wife, Mr Thompson,' he went on deliberately. 'One son. One daughter. I've been using supernatural means to track them down. And I think my wife is in North London. Somewhere near. But guarded.'

'By the dogs . . .' Rosa Thompson murmured. She was staring at him wide-eyed. For a moment she had seemed not to believe him, but Brady could intuit that his briefly stated agony had struck a chord with her. Her husband, too, was looking solemn, a little concerned.

Brady nodded. 'By the dogs,' he agreed.

'They're witch dogs,' Mr Thompson said suddenly. 'Our boy used charms to try and turn around a Hag. A Witch. So he must have seen the Witch who runs the dogs. Mister, I still ain't sure of you, but I'm sure of one thing. Our son looked at a book that *no one* should look at. If the police get to find that book, or ask questions, there's going to be a war in London that'll leave a bloodier wake than you can imagine. You ask me to believe you. OK. I ask you to believe me . . .' He had stepped closer to Brady, his face wet with perspiration, his deep eyes gleaming with an intensity that Brady could not ignore. 'What we tell you. What we show you. You keep to yourself. I ain't afraid of the police, and under normal circumstances I'd be with them now, asking them to help look for my kids. But I can't, mister. I can't risk the *hunganzi* . . .'

The name meant nothing to Brady . . . except that . . . except that a voodoo priest was called a *hungan*. He remembered that, now. So the *hunganzi* was –

'A book?'

'*The* book,' Thompson said. 'And that's all I'm going to say.' He looked around, up and down the street. Then to Brady: 'There's police out the front, you say? How about the back?'

'I don't know.'

'Let's try it, then. Come on. Quick.'

A few minutes later they were walking through the small, crowded back garden of the Thompsons' house. Rosamund let them in and they crept quietly upstairs, keeping well away from the front windows. Brady was deeply intrigued by the nature of the *hunganzi*, but it was clear that Thompson was not going to oblige with more information.

In the boy's room, Brady saw the same charcoal designs, voodoo seals and symbols, with which Ritchie's room had been decorated. Thompson was grim, almost angry, as he violently smudged one of the more grotesque images. 'He got it wrong. All the charms, he got them wrong. That's dangerous. That's why nobody should meddle.'

Rosamund stood in the doorway, clutching her hand-bag, watching the two men, staring at the walls.

Brady said, 'He got them wrong at Ritchie's house too. The boy's dead.'

Thompson glanced round at Rosamund, who briefly closed her eyes when she heard the news. 'We thought as much,' she said, after a moment. 'We went there early this morning. About one o'clock . . . When I discovered that Errol and Pippa were gone. I thought they might have gone back to Ritchie's. We saw the police. We guessed something bad had happened.'

Thompson said, 'We've been everywhere we know they go to play. We've been searching all night. We've also been for help of a different sort, help from certain people. But it's hard, Brady. Hard. If I tell . . . if I tell them about this, about Errol looking at the *hunganzi* . . . '

His gaze suddenly became haunted, terrified.

'Will they kill you?' Brady said quietly.

'Not entirely . . .' Thompson whispered. 'The body will live.'

Rosamund walked quickly to her husband and hugged him. Brady, trying not to think too hard about what the man had just implied, watched the two of them, registering their growing despair, their fear, their help-lessness.

It was a feeling he knew all too well.

He said, 'Ritchie's father suggested that their stomping-ground covered a very wide area . . .'

Thompson nodded, sniffing very loudly and breaking the hug with Rosamund. 'That's right. They've got bikes. I don't let them go too far south, too close to the city centre. But they've got hide-outs over a mile away. I know a few, but they play the game of secrets . . . I mean, why not? Secret hide-outs, special places. I did it as a child. They fly kites on Primrose Hill. I won't let them on the West Heath, Hampstead Heath. They're on their honour not to go there. But I saw them once walking along the Finchley Road, and *that's* a mile away.' He laughed bitterly. 'Where do we start to look?'

Rosamund sat down on her son's bed and tears spilled from her eyes. 'What's going on?' she murmured. What could they have done? Why *our* kids?'

'It's not just your kids,' Brady said. 'An Irish boy a few days ago. The Hughes boy. Who else? Who else might be in danger?'

Thompson thought for a moment, then said, 'The Cronin boy. Gerry Cronin. He was the other member of their gang. Wild imaginations, all of them. But Gerry had a lot of pocket money, and he always had the comics and toys that made the others envious. He had a video, a cassette player, even a TV in his room. So he used to tell Errol, anyhow.'

The boys were a gang; they played and roamed over an area of London that was quite dauntingly large, considering the number of streets, parks and allotments that were crowded into that space. At some time during the preceding week they had stumbled upon . . . upon what? *Something* that had got them into trouble.

Had that something been the house where Alison was guarded?

Or had the black dogs merely been attracted to the boys as they mucked about with black magic? It was not an unfamiliar situation to Brady. He had read of at least two cases where children playing – in those instances with Ouija-boards – had attracted supernatural elements to their rooms, and suffered in consequence.

There was another decision for Brady to make: should he mention Arachne to the Thompsons, or not? He was too wise, too hard-bitten now, to trust *anyone* involved in any way with magic, or the secret arts, no matter how innocent they might seem.

To ask them about Arachne might be to alert them – if they were involved. Not to ask might be to miss a clue, no matter how small.

A decision.

'You won't show me this book of yours?' he asked. Thompson shook his head.

'I can't. I swore an oath in blood to guard it. There are many books in London – books in all cities where the people are. One book for one parish. It's an honour to have the *hunganzi*. Mister – you wouldn't be interested in what it has in it, anyway. It's not – excuse me for the expression – "white man's magic": different people, different charms, different way of ghosts.'

He stopped talking, a little embarrassed perhaps. 'Sorry,' he added.

'Not necessary,' Brady said with a shrug. 'But you also don't even want me to *mention* the *hunganzi* . . .'

'I've already told you more than is safe to tell.'

'It's safe with me,' Brady reassured him. He walked over to Flynn's desk and asked, 'May I?' When Rosamund nodded he flipped open the lid and found what he was after – a piece of charcoal. The desk was full of comics, school-books, plastic guns – and a Memorex tape, marked with a yellow radioactive-warning label. In childish handwriting, across the yellow disc, were the words: *Death Unit 2000: Top Security!*

Brady picked the tape up and smiled, then placed it on top of the desk before he turned to the wall.

'Excuse the extra damage . . .' he said, 'but did you ever see this before?' And he drew the symbol of a spider. The Thompsons knew what it was, of course, but they didn't understand its significance.

Brady drew the classical Labyrinth, the double entwined spiral that represented the maze where Theseus had sought the Minotaur. 'How about this? Familiar?'

'A puzzle?' Rosamund shook her head. 'No.'

Thompson just shrugged.

Brady said, 'I'll keep quiet about the *hunganzi*. You do me the same favour?'

'Sure.'

'Does the word Arachne mean anything?'

Nothing, they said. And Brady, watching them hard, couldn't help but believe them. But that didn't mean that

Flynn himself – or Errol, as his parents called him – hadn't encountered, or wasn't familiar with, Arachne.

And he would *still* have loved to have seen what Thompson meant by a *hunganzi* book.

Rosamund Thompson had noticed the cassette tape and picked it up. 'Where did you get this?' she asked. Slightly surprised, Brady said, 'From his desk. Death Unit 2000 – that must be their gang. Yes?'

The woman nodded. 'Death Unit 2000,' she repeated. Then bitterly: 'Death, guns, death, mutants, death, zombies . . . always *death*. Always the bad. Never beauty. *Never a decent book!*' She slammed the tape down, angry and suddenly upset. Thompson went to her and rested his hands on her shoulders.

'Easy, Rosa. They'll be back. They'll be safe, and they'll be back.'

'It's polluted them, Johnny. Their minds, their feelings, violence and guns, and killing. We should have been firmer. We should have known.'

There was a tape deck in the corner, a small battered Japanese unit, very dusty. Brady picked up the tape from where she'd thrown it and put it into the machine. Switching it on he heard a boy's voice:

' . . . *about what happened to Tip? Trooper Flynn?*'

A second voice: '*He was running away from the Mutie Wasteland. He was very frightened when I saw him last.*'

'*Did he say what'd scared him?*'

'*He said . . . he said he'd found a river. That's it. A river. He said he'd been searching for Mutants and found a hidden doorway . . .*'

Brady switched the tape off. 'Is that your boy?'

Thompson nodded grimly.

Brady ejected the cassette and stared at it, wondering . . .

'Could I borrow this?'

'Why?' Thompson said quietly.

'I don't know. Maybe they saw something. Down in the sewers, perhaps. This seems to be a record of a meeting. Maybe the last meeting. There might be a clue on it, something about what they found . . .'

Thompson left Rosamund and walked over to Brady. He took the tape, put it back in the unit and ran it back to the beginning.

'That's my son. That voice. If . . . if he *doesn't* come back, this may be all we've got. So I'll keep the tape, if it's all the same to you. But you're welcome to listen to it through. We'll listen together. If you're right, if they hint at where they went on Saturday, that'll help us too.'

He switched the tape to *play*. Brady nodded quickly, then dropped to a crouch to listen to the last formal briefing of Death Unit 2000.

8

'How's your friend, by the way?' Françoise asked. 'I meant to ask you earlier.'

She was watching Andrew Haddingham as he slaved over a deep dish of green pasta, tossing it with a Gorgonzola and ham sauce. He was in his shirt-sleeves, his grey hair slightly tousled from the journey to his house from the Hillingvale Research Centre, during which he'd had his window open all the time. The kitchen of the small but tastefully decorated country house was hot, slightly steamy. He wore a white apron on which was a cartoon of an unshaven, greasy man in a chef's outfit, an evil stereotype of a Gallic cook, violently chopping up a piece of meat. The 'chef' wore an apron on which was printed 'I speet in your gravy'. It was an odd, and oddly hysterical, manifestation of the solemn man's latent sense of humour.

He frowned and glanced up at her, strands of tagliatelle caught between two serving spoons.

'Which friend is that?'

'Daniel Brady.'

'Oh. Right. Dan.' He went back to mixing sauce and pasta thoroughly. 'I'm not sure. I haven't seen him for a couple of months, now. Pass the pepper, would you?'

Françoise obliged, then prowled around the kitchen, inspecting the oddities on the spice shelf, the horrors in the vegetable rack, the obscenities that masqueraded as cheese in England, and finally . . . the wine.

It was red. It was from Sainsbury's. She felt weak at the knees. She told him so.

'Don't knock it,' Haddingham said. 'Good stuff is Sainsbury's wine. Good value.'

'It's the laxative value that worries me,' she said as she put the bottle down again.

'That's not a very nice thing to say . . .'

'I'm sorry. After the trouble I've given you today, you're right.' She came up behind him and peered at the concoction. 'It smells wonderful.'

'Tastes divine. Ninety per cent of my body-weight comprises pizza and pasta; m'dear, I'm a *pasta masta* at such things.'

'Groan!' She pinched his backside. 'Hurry up. I'm hungry.'

Haddingham had almost dropped the whole dish – in shock. He stared at her as she went through to the dining-room, carrying the red wine between two fingers, as if carrying a dustbin bag. 'You know what I've come to like about you?' he called, as he followed her, carrying the dish, the pepper and the small bowl of tossed salad.

'No. What?'

'You're so . . . so indescribably . . . *French*!'

They ate by the light of a single wall-lamp, and the small room was cosy, familiar. Françoise sat with her back to the open fireplace, pleased with the food, and now not at all unhappy with the wine.

Behind her, on the mantelpiece, the statuette of the moon goddess watched them with the eyes of the child in its belly. It was a dark, sinister shape, lying on its side. Occasionally, Haddingham glanced at it. Françoise was aware of it all the time, but not in the psychic way she had experienced that morning . . .

The afternoon session had been a failure, and she still felt very embarrassed about it. After the power – after the *horror* of the morning session, she had been unable to sense anything from the statuette as she had sat, surrounded by recording and filming equipment, in the MoD laboratories at Hillingvale. She had apologised, but Andrew had been fatalistic:

The offer for supper still stood, he had said to her. And with both cars loaded up with Ministry equipment, they had come to Andrew's house – for food, and another attempt.

The dark stone waited in the same room as them.

It watched . . .

'Why do you ask about Dan, by the way?' Haddingham asked, as he helped himself to seconds.

Françoise shrugged. In the half-light she looked very mysterious, very attractive. Her eyes gleamed, her body-scent was subtle but very provocative to the older man. 'I woke this morning thinking of him,' she said. 'I wondered if he'd had any luck with . . . his family, with finding them.'

Haddingham shook his head. 'No, not yet. But for Dan it's just a matter of time. He'll find them. One way or another.'

'He'll die to find them, you mean . . .'

With a quick, sad glance at Françoise, Haddingham agreed. 'He's put too much into finding them. If they're dead, then it will be by death that he will join them. But he still clings to the hope that all of them are alive.'

'I hope they are too,' she said softly.

After a moment, she brightened. 'This is very good. Fattening, but good.'

'We do our best,' Haddingham said, with a gracious little bow.

She stared at him. 'Why did you never marry? Or is that too personal?'

Haddingham leaned towards her, eyes gleaming. 'Why didn't *you*?'

'I did,' she said.

'So did I. Years ago.'

'Mine didn't last,' Françoise added.

'Mine ended badly too.'

'My husband died. My Antoine died. That's bad, but not the way you mean.'

'Oh.' Haddingham leaned back and looked thoughtful, a little crestfallen. 'I'm sorry.'

'I'm sorry too. No one else ever came along?'

'I've had my wild nights. And hungover days –'

'Me too.'

'You're with that American now, is that right?'

Françoise laughed. 'Liam Kline. Yes. For a while.' She shrugged. 'A short while. A long while. I don't know. I like him. I *love* him. But Antoine was special . . .' She toyed with the remnants of her pasta, then repeated softly, 'I don't know. Sometimes – very rarely – but sometimes someone comes into your life who becomes so much a *part* of your life that – well . . .'

'When they go, something goes with them.'

She nodded, staring down at the plate, still fiddling with her fork. 'Antoine was my life. God! I was so much a part of him! Him of me. I'm still empty . . . I don't think I'll ever be . . . I don't think I could ever be the way I was. Not again.'

She looked up at Haddingham. He was solemn; watching her. Listening. She said, 'Is that why you never married again?'

With a shrug: 'I don't know. I got older. I got involved with my work. And with the paranormal. I grope a secretary or two at Christmas, date a widow or two every summer. Risk heart attack, worry about my performance. Get depressed. Realise that unless I meet another – well, another *me*, a female me, I'm likely to be a single man for all the rest of my days.'

'A bachelor gay . . .'

'Certainly not!'

'I didn't mean –' She laughed. 'A bachelor lazy, anyway. You're not making enough effort.'

'True. I depend on friends a lot.'

'And get depressed when you betray them –'

He looked at her sharply. 'I beg your pardon?'

'Like Brady . . .' she began.

And then she realised what she had done.

'Oh my God. Oh God, Andrew. I'm sorry, I'm really sorry.'

The whole room became hot. She felt on fire. Had-

dingham's face was bright red, a flush of embarrassment
and of anger. He stared at her, not fully understanding, but
aware that she had – in some way – been reading him, been
intuiting him. The fork, or the table, or the ambience, or
just her closeness – she had tuned into him!

For her part, Françoise was horrified at her failure to
control her power. She had done the thing that had
haunted her for all of her childhood, and had become a
nuisance during her adult life. She had done the thing that
she had promised she would never do, the betrayal that
was not *deliberate*, but which – innocently occurring or
not – had caused her such terrible alienation in her life.

She had expressed aloud a feeling she had had about
someone; she had broken a trust with herself. Her power
to 'feel' gave her insight, intuition, and simple *facts* about
people, and for more than twenty years she had disciplined
herself to at least not betray that she *knew*.

How stupid!

Her fever of angry embarrassment grew. With it, panic
and discomfort from Andrew. He radiated emotion like a
beacon. He was totally confused.

'I suppose I have . . .' he said.

'Andrew. Don't say anything. It's *my* fault. And I'm
sorry . . . '

'No. No it isn't. It's all right, Françoise. You're right. I
have betrayed him.'

'Andrew –'

'I could have done so much for him. When Dan left
Hillingvale, I was his immediate superior. I could have
helped more. I could have got him help. I could have
arranged money for him – I could have left the place
myself and helped him. My God. Yes. I betrayed him by
fear. I left him to do everything alone, to face it all alone –
without family, without income, without *understanding*.
No wonder he's so bitter. No wonder he's changed. He's a
man alone, despite – despite me, and Angela Huxley. And
you. The one thing he never got was just the feeling that
. . . that *someone*, a *friend*, would give up everything to
help . . .'

'The American did,' Françoise said softly. 'She gave up her life.'

'Yes,' Haddingham agreed uncertainly. 'Yes. She did. But she wasn't someone whom he'd known before. Not a friend.'

Françoise watched him intently, perplexed by his despair, puzzled by his abrupt shift in mood. It was so extreme. He was suddenly so *very* upset.

But before she could speak again . . .

Haddingham looked up, a sudden, shocked movement. And she heard it too. Loud. Sinister . . .

The sound of a slow, steady heartbeat!

It was coming from behind her. She stood up quickly, knocking her chair over, and walked rapidly across the room, almost reluctant to look at the grotesque statue. Andrew came with her, backing away from the table, his serviette still tucked into the waistband of his trousers. They stood by the wall together and watched the dark stone.

The heartbeat grew stronger. It seemed to pump through the air itself, and Haddingham's eardrums responded to pressure-change in the room.

'What's *started* this?' he whispered. .

'Me,' Françoise said. 'My embarrassment. A moment of high emotion – I've known this to happen before.'

'It's so loud. And the damned equipment isn't set up!'

He started to move across the room, to get at least a tape-recorder running, to document the ghostly life-beat. But as he began to walk, he was stopped. It was as if a hand pressed him back. He struggled forward, but a pressure on his chest kept him stationary. There was pressure on his face and on his legs. He was being stifled by something . . .

He heard a strange sound above the heartbeat: the sound of horses, hundreds of horses, cantering towards him. Their harnesses rattled. They snorted impatiently as the canter became a gallop. The human cries he could hear were the triumphal screams of warriors, as they bore down upon him in the grey light.

Silver light . . .

Bright glow!

The room had become icy. Françoise's breath frosted in the air in front of her as she stood and watched the light emanating from the goddess stone. The sound of the horses was loud and frightening. She was among them, running *with* them. She could feel the wind in her hair, the bumping of her small chariot on the stony ground. She could smell the rank sweat of animals, and the ash scent of burning.

The goddess stone was in the air before her. It had risen from the mantelpiece and now floated upright a few feet from the ground, bathed in light. A long tendril of silver energy gradually extended from the parted lips of the child's face in its belly. The eyes of the child were open and seemed to watch. The cord of silver rope stretched out across the room, towards the window, a glistening snake, writhing and feeling its way to the outside.

It was being called. There was no other explanation for the eerie sense of *reaching* that Françoise was experiencing. The stone was being summoned. It was searching for the way to the outside; the power within it was awakening. It had risen from slumber and needed to *unite* . . .

To join again . . .

To be *whole* again.

Françoise took a step forward, staggering slightly. Her entire body racked with cold, her limbs aching with the chill. The room was now a single glare of silver light, a blinding moonglow that made her eyes water. Other tendrils of energy came from the stone; they reached towards her, and where they touched, her skin burned. The eyes of the child watched her, and now the expression in them was malevolent. The broken neck of the figure seemed to glisten with blood. The breasts of the statue rose and fell as the figure breathed; the leg moved, the arms moved, the belly swelled up, the child's mouth opened wider.

It was like a quivering spider, the flexing strands of silver stretching out like legs from the broken body. The statue began to drift towards the window, and Françoise could *feel* the entity within it murmuring in its half-conscious state, stirring as it awakened . . .

It was female. It was old. It was all-loving, all-embracing. It watched from the stone, and Françoise touched its confusion for a moment –

Touched –

Whole again. Alive again. Powerful. So long in the dark. So long to wait. Resurrection now. Flesh again. Awake. The moon again. The time of the moon is coming!

'NO!' Françoise screamed. She had been suddenly overwhelmed by desperate, sickening fear. Laughter came from the stone; age-old, cruel laughter. The embryo squirmed and poked at her with its shining legs of moon-stuff. Her skin burned. Her heart froze. Her mouth was caught open and something foul, some awful object, licked around inside, then touched her eyes, her nose, her breasts. Then withdrew . . .

With a sudden shocking impact, and the shattering of glass, the stone figure was gone from the room. The light vanished too, and only the dim yellow lamp illuminated the two shaken figures of Françoise and Haddingham. Warmth crept back to the place, and Haddingham could move again. He walked slowly to the broken window and stared out into the night.

He noticed that the moon was almost full.

Then he turned back to where Françoise was huddled on the floor, retching violently into his wastepaper bin.

Afterwards, she slept for a while, curled up on the settee, covered by a blanket. Haddingham went about the house setting up some very simple defences against psychic and elemental attack. That done, he crept quietly back to the lounge and sat and watched the sleeping woman for a while.

Soon, he himself dozed off.

He woke at about midnight, feeling cold and very disorientated. He could hear Françoise in the hallway, speaking softly on the phone, probably to her American friend, Liam. She was saying that she was drained and very shaken-up. She would be home the following morning.

When she came back into the lounge, the blanket wrapped about her shoulders like a Sioux Indian, she smiled and apologised to Haddingham.

'I didn't mean to wake you. I used your phone. I hope that was all right.'

'That's fine.'

Haddingham climbed to his feet and nodded good-night to her. He hesitated, then, and said, 'Did I really see a cold stone object take on a life of its own?'

'Yes. You did.'

He stared at her. 'Something snatched it away.'

'It went to find – to find the other parts of its body, I think.'

'There was something more than memory locked inside it.'

'Yes,' she said, and shuddered violently. 'A lot more.'

He turned from her. 'Tell me about it in the morning. The irrational always seems much more acceptable over breakfast.'

In this way, then, it was not until the following day, when Dan Brady was already in London, that Haddingham discovered the link between the statue and Brady's quest, a link that he made when Françoise used two simple, telling phrases.

'Something in the stone is awakening. Something is being resurrected.'

9

An hour after Dan had left for London, Anita Herbert got up, bathed, then performed her daily ritual, walking the grounds of Brook's Corner, checking the defences. She opened a pathway to the outside so that Ellen Bancroft, drifting in the invisible substance of the Otherworld, could see 'beyond'.

Almost immediately there was an atmosphere of agitation in the house, and Anita drew back from the window, frowning. Her pulse-beat quickened, and she stared at the lounge, looking slightly towards the ceiling as if Ellen – a ghost – would come floating down from the plasterboard.

Whenever Ellen was worried or upset, there were two physical manifestations of that anxiety that never failed to occur: a wind blew down the chimney, disturbing the ash and fire-litter in the grate; and the curtains shifted in an unfelt breeze, an eerie activity that gave simple cloth drapes the illusion of life.

This manifestation could occur throughout the house, but was usually centred on the lounge, the room in which the grotesque elemental had killed Ellen, seven months or so before. The temperature dropped slightly at the same time, and the room became a crisp, cool area; at the same time, any conscious mind present would sharpen, become intensely focused, as if the spiritual energy of the dead woman had washed the awareness clean.

Anita stood, now, and watched the room shift and shudder, listening to the rustling of wind in the grate, waiting for some sign that would indicate the nature of the disturbance.

Distantly, a woman called. She looked outside, to the

dark stand of trees. The woman's voice sounded again, calling . . . hailing her.

Anita took an involuntary step towards the open french windows. They closed loudly, startling her.

That was a good enough sign from Ellen. Anita opened the doors again and quickly broke the path across the *mazon*, sealing the house behind its defences.

As she straightened up, the sweet voice called to her; the woman was at the bottom of the garden, beyond the wall. The words she called were simple: 'Come here! Come *here*. Quickly. I'm here! Come and talk to me.'

Every hair on Anita's body pricked at her skin and she shivered violently, curious yet filled with a terror that was – in its way – quite irrational. She recognised well enough that Ellen was warning her against pursuing the sound of that voice.

'Come *here*! Oh *please* come and talk to me . . .'

The voice was so plaintive, so gentle, so pleading.

Anita peered hard through the lounge window, but could only see the apple trees and the Talisman Wall at the bottom of the garden. Her skin continued to react with a mixture of fear and cold. Ellen's icy fingers tugged at her, pulled her deeper into the room. Papers rustled on the table. Objects fell loudly from shelves upstairs; a window banged loudly and repeatedly.

'Are you there? Is *anybody* there? Anita. *Anita*!'

At the sound of her name, Anita shivered violently and felt a powerful draw towards the window. She was frozen, for a moment, face pressed against the glass, her breath steaming the cold glass and misting up her vision.

Behind her, then, the telephone began to ring. She turned and stared at it, but her limbs were like lead. The voice still echoed in her mind, calling her name so desperately. She took a step towards the table where the phone stood, and slowly the jarring sound of its bell grew louder, and broke through the trance that had possessed her.

Suddenly she ran for the phone and snatched it from the cradle. But there was just silence at the other end, and then the dialling tone.

Replacing the receiver, she went quickly upstairs and walked along the landing. From its window she could see across the trees and the lawn to the distant woodland, and the area of rough land in between.

The woman stood there, just the other side of the wall, waving to her. She was wearing a simple white dress, a summer dress, quite unsuitable to the cold, grey weather. Around her neck was tied a black scarf. She had long, dark hair which was not styled, but hung fairly limply around her shoulders.

From this distance it was hard to see her face clearly, but she was familiar; Anita felt that she knew her, had seen her before . . .

She opened the landing window and leaned out.

'Come here!' the woman called. 'Please *please* come and talk to me. Anita . . . *please* come . . .'

There was a hand on her arm, an invisible hand. The fingers squeezed hard, almost painfully. They tugged at her. Warm breath in her face almost shaped into words.

Don't don't don't. Trap trap trap.

'Aneeeeetaaaa . . .'

The woman in the field was hailing her, her voice an eerie howling. She waved. Wind blew her white dress. The quality of the voice changed, becoming sharp, malevolent:

'An*ita*! *Nita*! *Nita*!'

Resist. Resist. Trap. Don't go.

'Anita. Oh *come, please.* Please!'

And gradually the woman's face became clear to Anita, and she realised why there was such a sense of familiarity . . .

It was Alison. It was Dan's wife, Alison. She was there, in the field, looking perhaps just as she had been when abducted nearly a year ago. Alison. Safe, alive. Alison Brady, desperate to get into the house, into the grounds, but perhaps kept at bay by the defences. Perhaps she was still tainted by the evil aura of those who had taken her. She couldn't get home. She was cold, she was frightened. She had escaped, and now wanted nothing more than to come into the warm, into safety.

Trap. Resist . . .

Ellen's mind-voice faded slowly, beaten back by the confusion of emotions that Anita was feeling. It was Alison out there. What would Alison think of Anita being in the house? Would she be angry? Where was Dan? He would have to know. Oh God, he would be so relieved, so happy . . .

Downstairs, the phone rang again. It might have been ringing in another world. Anita Herbert could hear it, but she remained fixed at the window, smiling into the distance, tugged both ways, torn between attraction and warning . . .

Then something inside her snapped. It was Dan. Dan was on the phone. The ringing was loud, now. She raced along the landing and into the bedroom, snatching the phone from its cradle.

She shouted, 'Quickly. Quickly Dan. She's here, she's home. Come back *now* . . .'

A man's voice answered her, but she ignored it, dropping the receiver onto the bed and running down the stairs, to the back door. Her heart was racing. She could hardly think. She ran down the garden, through the trees, and leapt up onto the wall, hanging on as best she could as she peered over into the rough field.

Alison was standing there, smiling.

'Is it really you?' Anita shouted. 'Are you Alison?'

'Where's Dan?' Alison asked.

'He'll be here. Very soon. Are the psychic defences bothering you?'

Alison held out her hand, beckoning Anita. In the house, a few yards behind her, a window broke and an eerie wail, like a cry of grief, echoed down the garden. It gave Anita a moment's pause, then Alison's smile reassured her. Overwhelmed by joy, completely possessed by the magnetism of the woman in the field, Anita scrambled over the wall and reached out to take Alison's hand.

They ran quickly towards the woods, but before quite reaching them they stopped.

'What are we doing?' Anita asked, breathless.

'This is the place,' Alison said, and looked down at the ground. The trees were a few yards away, and Anita thought she could hear a slight, furtive movement among them.

'What place?'

Alison stared at her, eyes bright, almost depthless.

'The place where the old roads crossed,' she said. 'The place of ghosts. Look . . . look at the house . . .'

Anita turned to glance towards the wall and garden of Brook's Corner. What she saw there made her gasp with shock . . .

The house as she knew it was gone, the wall too, and the trees. Standing there, below a lowering sky, slightly screened by small, yellow-leaved trees, was a Roman villa, its red-tiled roof bright, its main building obscured behind a wooden palisade. Anita was standing on a stone road that ran close by to the villa and stretched away into the distance, towards London. The landscape was bare, save for a few dense stands of trees. Where she was standing, a second road, more of a rough track, cut across the first. The landscape was totally different, the weather different . . . It was a strangely remote place, and the very air seemed charged with the peculiar calm that precedes a terrible storm.

In the distance, towards London, there seemed to be a darkness, a dull, distant thunder. Dust clouds rose into the sky. Light flashed on a thousand small, bright objects, moving rapidly across the wide land, approaching the place where Anita stood shocked by this strange vision . . .

'What does it mean?' she asked Alison, and turned to the woman.

Her scream of shock and horror was shrill and short, stifled by the rough hand that clamped across her mouth as she was grabbed from behind. The fingers of the hand were filthy, the nails long and black, but a woman's hand, a strong, work-hardened hand. She was lifted from the ground and she felt a rope slip around her neck and tighten, cutting into her skin, pressing agonisingly hard against her Adam's apple.

Where Alison had been standing there was something that might once have been a woman, but which was now far more like a corpse. Clothed in ragged, disintegrating robes, its hair a long, lank fall of dirty grey, the hag grinned at her through lips that were yellowed and drawn. Only the eyes in the skull-like face retained life, a shining, piercing life. The hag watched the struggling girl, and reached a bony, withered hand to touch Anita's forehead.

Nearby, out of sight, a dog growled, loud and savage. The tension on her neck increased, and she felt herself tugged from the ground as her weight was taken on the rope. The hand released her mouth and she tried to scream, but the sound was choked from her. Her eyes streamed tears, but then cleared as the pressure was relaxed and her feet touched the ground again. Rough hands bound her wrists behind her back. Other female shapes moved across her vision, a younger woman, proudly presented, magnificently built. And a girl, tall and strikingly thin, her face a sweet mask of innocence, except when she stepped forward and smiled at the slowly strangling girl . . . in the eyes, in the smile, was evil of a sort that made the last flutters of hope in Anita's breast quieten down and abandon her.

'Where's . . . Alison . . .' she gasped, conscious of the growing throb of pain in her head and the darkening of her vision. She didn't know if she had even uttered sound. She found courage and strength, and determined to fight, and by fighting, she clung to sanity and consciousness.

'Where . . . is . . . she . . .?'

The corpse face came closer, breathing fetid fumes into her nostrils, shaking its head from side to side as the brilliantly dark eyes watched her from the decaying bone. Then, in Alison Brady's voice, it laughed and murmured, 'She is where the greatest of us waits to rise from sleep. I'm here, Dan. Here I am, Dan-Danny-Dan. Oh come to me, come to me . . .'

More laughter, breaking the mocking flow of words.

'Brady . . . will . . . kill . . . you . . .' Anita gasped, her lips swelling as the pressure in her head and face increased.

Still her toes just touched the ground, enabling her to cling to life. As she twisted and swung slightly she could see that she was suspended from a crude cross-armed gibbet, standing right in the apex of the crossroads.

The hag's laughter rattled in her throat. 'He will be dead before he ever finds the shrine. The woman is on the hill by the city. I guard her, and when she becomes the goddess I shall be her guardian still. You have no hope . . .'

'You don't know how strong he is,' Anita cried, her voice a strangled whine. Distantly, the thunder came closer, and from the villa nearby she heard the sound of screaming . . .

For a minute or so, then, she was treated to a bizarre and horrific spectacle. The hag drew back, the three women turned from her and peered across the illusory landscape towards the Roman building, and the two terrified people who had been dragged out to stand by the road. They were husband and wife, he dressed in a toga with short, dark trousers below, she clad in glorious red and green robes. They were in their middle age and they struggled in the grip of tall, near-naked men with bodies smeared with white and blue paint, and hair standing stiffly on their heads, like the quills of porcupines.

From the direction of the thunder came an army of men, led by a flame-haired woman in a small chariot. Her cloak flapped widely behind her as she sped towards the villa, a great war-spear in her hand, her red hair billowing about her regal head as she watched the distant scene.

The host of men surrounded the villa, yelling and chanting, uttering weird, ululating cries. Many of them climbed down from their chariots and scaled the walls into the gardens. Smoke rose from behind those walls, and the drum of horses was drowned by the repeated piercing cries of children dying within.

In two swift motions, too fast for Anita to follow, the heads of the matron and her husband were detached from their bodies. The queen held that of the man by its short hair, and the chariot came towards the crossroads. The red-haired warrior queen looked sneeringly down at

140

Anita, then with a single, vicious movement impaled the head on the spear she carried, before driving the sharpened end of the haft into the ground beside the chariot. The grim, gaping trophy watched the gasping girl through dulled eyes.

A moment later the chariot was gone, and the huge army of men, women and baggage-carts was streaming past the crossroads, heading north.

In too much pain to worry about what she had seen, and why, Anita began to struggle in her bonds. A moment later she was tugged from the ground, and the rope bit deeply into her neck, cutting off her breath, cutting off the flow of blood.

The last thing she was aware of was that powerful hands had gripped her body and were spinning her on the gibbet, lifting her higher, humiliating her further . . .

Then there was just the merciful numbness and darkness of dying.

From a hundred yards away, Brady watched the house, the engine of his Land-Rover idling. There was a car parked outside Brook's Corner. He recognised it, but for a moment couldn't think from where. He was tired. It was late morning. His encounter with the Hughes and Thompson families had left him more confused than enlightened, and he needed to think.

He didn't want visitors.

And then he realised whose car it was. Andrew Haddingham had changed his Ford Escort for a new model in April. The Hillingvale Research Centre sticker was easily seen in the rear window.

Haddingham. A trusted friend, and always welcome. But what did he *want*, Brady wondered?

He drove forward and turned into the drive, slowing only to look again, and with no diminishing of his apprehension, at the crudely drawn hex-symbols on the outer face of the Talisman Wall.

As he climbed from the Land-Rover, the front door of

141

his house opened and Haddingham, looking pale and worried, stepped out to greet him.

'Thank God you've come back,' he said, and Brady frowned as he shook hands.

'Nice to see you, Andrew. To what do I owe – ?'

Haddingham cut him short, taking his arm and almost pulling him into the house. 'It's Anita . . .'

'Anita?'

'The trouble with this damn place is I never know what to do for the best. God, what a mess . . .'

Brady hesitated, tugging at the older man. 'Is she all right?'

'I don't know. I think so. Françoise Jeury is with her. You remember her?'

'Yes. I do.'

They raced up the stairs to the main bedroom. Françoise rose solemnly to her feet at the bedside as Brady came in.

'Oh my God,' he said as he saw the girl. 'What happened?'

'Someone tried to hang her,' Françoise said. 'In the woodland behind the house. She's still alive. But we *must* have a doctor.'

Anita's face was grey, her lips still swollen and puffy. A vicious rope-burn ran around her neck, and the flesh was depressed by almost half an inch. The girl's breathing was laboured, a hissing gasp as she struggled to suck air through her wounded windpipe. Her hands clutched at the duvet on which she was lying. As Brady watched, so her eyes flickered open. All he saw were the blood-congested whites.

'We *must* have a doctor,' Françoise said again.

'Of course. There's a number in the book by the downstairs phone.'

Haddingham ran down to fetch the help needed. Brady couldn't blame him for hesitating. Brook's Corner was not a place where normal humanitarian decisions could be easily made.

'We rang this morning,' Françoise said. 'First there was

142

no answer. Then the girl answered, but sounded upset. So we came over anyway. The house was empty, but your ghost was very agitated. I walked upstairs and from the landing saw the girl hanging from a tree. We only just got there in time, I think. She was still struggling as we got her down, but she was very weak.'

The news filled Brady with dread. He watched the unconscious girl. 'But who – who would *do* that? And why? What's Anita to them?'

Françoise made a sound like a snort of irritation. 'Who do you think?'

Brady stared at her. After a moment he said, 'I don't think I *want* to think . . .'

Anita made a sudden hissing sound, and her lips moved. Brady leaned close to her, trying to hear if she was speaking. He frowned. After a moment he began to recognise the rasped words, and repeated them aloud: 'The place of ghosts. Anita . . . *Anita*. Can you hear me? What does it mean? What do you mean? Where is the place of ghosts?'

But she had lapsed into strained silence again, and Brady straightened up. 'Has she said anything else?'

Françoise nodded solemnly. 'She keeps repeating that expression. And something else. She says, "The hill by city". Does that mean anything to you?'

'It might,' Brady replied softly. And then, with a sigh almost of despair, he said, 'Arachne . . .' He sat down next to Anita, resting his hand gently on her cold face. 'I wondered when they would strike again. Now I *know* they're involved . . .'

Françoise frowned quickly. 'Involved? Involved with what?'

Glancing up, Brady said, 'It's a complicated story. I've been searching for Alison in London. I'm sure she's there . . .'

'London's a big place.'

'I know. I've narrowed the hunt down. Arachne are guarding her, though, and I think the guardians have been disturbed.'

With a wry little laugh, the Frenchwoman said, 'Well I'm afraid the story's about to get *more* complicated. Let me tell you what Andrew and I have just found . . .'

The doctor came and went. He was satisfied that Anita was in no danger, but very dissatisfied with Brady's refusal to let her be taken to hospital, and with his request that the doctor did *not* report the attack.

They compromised.

The doctor would not contact the police for six hours. He would return at that time, check the girl again and then call Andrew Sutherland.

Brady told Haddingham about Stefan Taber's death, then the two of them walked to the woodland, to the exact spot where Anita's body had been strung up. There was little to see now, save the cut length of rope. But when Haddingham had cut the girl down, he had heard the growl of a dog, close by and angry . . .

Now they sat around the table in the lounge, hands clasped in front of them, empty coffee mugs gathered at one side. The Nordic talisman that Brady usually wore was wrapped in linen and black silk and hidden in his office. Its presence unnerved the hypersensitive Françoise, and Brady had reluctantly agreed to remove it.

He had listened twice to a detailed account of exactly what Françoise had experienced and envisaged during her contact with the goddess statuette. He had told them of his own experiences. They sat, now, and let the linkages form, trying to find the truth among the profusion of horrific events and apparently unconnected contacts with the supernatural.

Firstly, there was Brady's absolute certainty that his wife was being held somewhere in North London. She was guarded by Arachne. They had a purpose in mind for her.

Secondly, when Brady had tried to locate her he had been attacked by a phantom hound. The same dog had pursued him all the way to Brook's Corner. And the same dog had almost certainly killed several boys who had – like Brady – disturbed them.

But the boys weren't looking for Alison. Was it possible, then, that whatever those phantoms were, they responded only to psychic disturbance – a mind, probing in their vicinity from its vantage-point on the British Telecom Tower; a boy mucking about with voodoo? Or had the boys *found* where Alison was being kept . . .?

Thirdly, both Angela Huxley and the ghost of Ellen Bancroft had been disturbed by a sensation of the coming of the moon. The moon. Three women. And – in Angela's case – a strong sense of sexual power. Brady had been unable to understand what this meant at the time. Now, and fourthly, he felt he comprehended it.

Arachne were raising the moon – the Moon Goddess – the power of the night.

Like Andrew Haddingham, Françoise's experienced awareness of the Moon Goddess being 'awakened and resurrected' bespoke *only* Arachne to Brady, and almost incontrovertibly so. The fire in the City of London that had allowed the excavation and release of the broken statuette had been the first step in resurrecting the two-thousand-year-old entity from its small stone tomb.

In the vision, Françoise had seen women – three women? Three priestesses? – and they had been standing on a hill to the north of a burning city. London had been burned in AD 61. Had that savagery been watched from the hill where now rows of terraced buildings housed families like the Hughes and Thompsons? A hill with nooks and crannies and a bloody history, where children, playing in waste ground, might have stumbled upon the more recent manifestations of that cruel past?

Françoise had sensed a river, an enclosed place.

Flynn Thompson – speaking on the tape – had referred to his friend, Aiden McGeary, having found a river. The rest of Death Unit 2000 had gone to search for that subterranean source. The place was in the 'Mutie Wasteland'. It could have been any one of hundreds of desolate overgrown patches of London in their wide, crowded patrol territory.

But it seemed self-evident that they had finally *found* the river . . .

And the guardian of that shrine had come to find them. Ritchie Hughes was dead. Gerry Cronin was missing. And the Thompson children had run away to hide . . .

Or had they, too, been found by now, and torn to pieces?

Raising the Moon Goddess; another source of magic for the growing power that was Arachne.

Brady remembered the shrine in Anerley, from his last encounter with Arachne just a few weeks before. Eight people, laid out like the legs of a spider, had been feeding another, embryonic force of ancient evil. The vision he now experienced was of Alison, similarly unconscious, her life essence slowly being tapped as the moon waxed, as the female entity grew in strength . . .

Their purpose is to resurrect a total magic, using the forces, demons and secret knowledge of all the different cultures of history. Total magic. Total eclipse. Their purpose is an Awakening. Their purpose is to control the World Mind . . .

Françoise said, 'If Alison is a part of a shrine, like the one you've described, then it is only just being set up. All of this is very recent.'

She was right, Brady realised. The statuette had only just been called out of the earth. When it was snatched from Haddingham's house, almost certainly it was the call of Arachne that had taken it. If they had been around before, then surely they would have taken the object from the museum.

Interesting . . .

That meant that perhaps, until recently, Arachne had not been active in the area. Alison had been guarded by the phantoms, ready for the time when a shrine would be established below the hill, near to an underground river. Coming alive at the magic call of its new Masters, the statuette had perhaps *caused* its own discovery. It was alive, it was aware . . . in its fabric was recorded much of its violent history, the object itself used to kill sacrificial victims, its heavily female form smeared with blood offerings. It had been kept by priestesses in a sacred, secret place. It contained the essence of the moon, the three faces of womanhood . . .

Yes. Of course. Brady now realised what the missing head must have shown. There was youth, peering innocently from the belly of the mature, fertile body – but the head would have been the head of a hag.

The moon in three parts. Poor Angela Huxley, touching the spirit of the tripartite goddess she had experienced raw fertility, the emotive sexual charge that had been so revered at a time when fertility was the gift of a deity!

Almost immediately he thought of what Flynn had been trying to do, using a charm to 'turn about a hag'. And his father had referred to the dogs as 'witch dogs'.

Wherever the fragment, the head of the statue, lay hidden, it was from that oldest and most evil of the three faces that the guardianship, and the haunting, was coming. They were dealing, indeed, with one of the darkest of the ancient earth forces: represented as the moon and sometimes – in some manifestations – associated with the horse, the awakening spirit was that of the Princess of Darkness.

Hecate herself!

'Hecate!' Haddingham said, and then understood. 'Of course. Tripartism. Young, mature, old. Persephone, Diana . . . the guardian of the Underworld, and of fertility. Hecate had black dogs as companions, and was malevolent in the extreme. She was the goddess of crossroads, and . . .' He broke off, staring through the wall towards the distant woodland. 'And of the gibbet!' he finished.

'Was Anita hanged at a crossroads?' Françoise asked.

Brady said, 'An old road used to run along where the edge of the wood is. Yes. And if a road had run past the villa that lies below the garden and part of the field, then where she was found would once have been a cross-roads . . .'

'The place of ghosts,' Haddingham whispered, shaking his head. 'Anita knew. Her executioner must have said it. Ghosts, gibbets, crossroads, the place of power of the black witches' deity. Some trivial manifestation of the greater power still locked in the stone has been guarding, and attacking, and haunting. If it could kill Taber at that sort of distance . . . if it could entrap Anita through the defences around Brook's Corner . . . the true power is almost too much to contemplate.'

Brady shook his head. 'The true power of the witch goddess, if that's what it is, is no power at all until it has been incubated, fed and awakened. We have to find it before that can happen.'

'Your lost Thompson children are the key,' Françoise said.

Brady added, 'Or the site, in the City, where the statue was found.'

'True. It might be a good idea to begin there. My talents might be useful . . .'

'But someone must stay with Anita,' Brady said, and smiled thinly as Haddingham rolled his eyes in silent, disappointed acceptance.

10

Forty miles away from Brook's Corner, two children explored the warren of dark rooms and passages that was their subterranean hide-out. Trog City, as they called it, was the old basement and storage area of a small industrial complex. The main building had been partially torn down, but the shells of offices and warehouses still poked ragged walls to the sky and formed an isolated, deserted patch of concrete and gravel that was a perfect children's playground.

'I'm still aching!' Pippa Thompson complained, as she followed her brother into another low-ceilinged, empty chamber. It had been an uncomfortable night. Flynn used his small pocket flashlight to check the place for any useful supplies, but the room was empty.

'Stop complaining,' he said.

'There's *got* to be a proper toilet *somewhere*,' the girl muttered. Flynn sighed. He was forced to agree. The one discomfort that was really, well, uncomfortable, was that there was no toilet facility in the stronghold. Both children felt very embarrassed at what they had had to do that morning.

'Nobody'll find us here,' Flynn said, changing the subject. He led the way back to their main camp area, and stepped inside the chalk circle he had marked on the floor. Light spilled into the cellars from several glass-covered grills above them. Throughout the dark underground these occasional shafts of brightness were welcome sights.

'Nobody and *nothing* will track us down.'

'I'm hungry,' Pippa said, standing watching her brother as the grey light bathed him.

'OK. Let's eat something. Anything you like. You choose.'

She went to the small pile of tinned supplies, crouched down and searched through them. But as fast as she had felt hungry, she lost her appetite. She picked up a comic, but let it fall. She stood up and shivered, staring up, through the concrete ceiling to the day outside.

'How long've we got to stay here, Flynn?'

'Until it's safe,' her brother said grimly.

'But how *long*? I don't want to stay here till *Christmas*. It's so *cold*.'

'Just a few days. And I'll go and scavenge for some more blankets. We'll be OK. We've got everything we need . . .'

'Except a toilet.'

'But everything to *survive*. We've got food, water and blankets. And we've got magic . . .'

He stepped from the circle and went over to the walls where he had inscribed the patterns and symbols from the *hunganzi* book. 'These charms will keep the hag and her hag-dogs at bay.'

'Mum said you'd got it all wrong,' Pippa said quietly, nervously.

'She would, wouldn't she,' Flynn retorted in defiance. 'But she was just trying to discourage us. No. These charms will turn the hag around. They're the right charms. Don't you worry.'

The girl shuddered, as if somehow intuiting the error in his words. 'I hope so,' she said. 'I really hope so . . .'

Andrew Haddingham followed the Land-Rover out into the road and watched it vanish into the distance. Then, with a nervous glance around him, he stepped back into the grounds of Brook's Corner and closed the iron gates, leaning on them for a moment as he quickly scanned the woodland on the far side of the road.

Back inside the house, he closed the front door and began to feel terribly anxious. He hadn't grasped, until now, just how much he disliked this place. There was absolute silence, of course, and yet . . . there was constant noise. There was a shuffling, whispering presence forever following him about as he walked from room to room. The doors always seemed to open slightly as he passed; the curtains were never still; parts of the house creaked as if someone was tiptoeing towards him. The only part of the house that was ever silent and still was where he stood any one time; and even then, it was as if a breath was being held, and he was being watched. When he moved on, that part of the house relaxed and breathed again, creaking and shuffling distractingly loudly.

Haddingham made himself a weak cup of coffee, which he then carried upstairs. He walked quietly along the landing and into the main bedroom, where Anita lay silently in the bed, her arms outside the covers.

He was not at all happy at being left as nursemaid. He felt he should have been with Brady and Françoise Jeury at the Walbrook Excavation. Dammit all . . . it was he who had *started* the investigation. Without him, Brady would never have made the connection between his own haunting and the reawakening of the lunar entity within the stone statue.

Grumbling to himself, he stared out of the window across the garden, sipping coffee and listening to Anita's breathing. She started to murmur, incoherent sounds, shapeless words. He walked over and peered closely at her, listening hard. But when he could make no sense of her dream-talk he shook his head and sat down on the end of the bed, still gazing thoughtfully at the daylight; still churning with irritation that he had been left behind . . .

And that he had so readily agreed to this secondary role.

He was second in command at Hillingvale! He knew more about psychic research than Uri Geller! He should have been with the other two, he should have been *leading* them.

He raised his cup to his lips, then hesitated.

Anita's murmuring had stopped.

He looked round and, with a start of surprise, realised that for the last few moments Anita had been sitting bolt upright in the bed, staring at him.

'You've changed since I last saw you.'

As he drove along the motorway to London, Brady had been reflecting that this was the third time he had made the trip to the City in less than thirty hours. At this rate he would do better to set up a base in London itself . . .

Françoise's words interrupted his idle thinking. He smiled, glanced at her and somehow grasped that for the last few miles she had been watching him very thoughtfully.

'In what way changed?' he asked.

'You're harder,' she said. 'And greyer . . .'

He ran a hand through his long, wiry hair and smiled ruefully. 'I thought it made me look distinguished.'

'It gives you an animal look,' she said. 'If I were to meet both you as you are now and you as you were six months ago . . . I don't think I'd recognise that I was with the same man.'

Brady slowed as he saw a police patrol car setting the pace in the slow lane. 'I'm very resigned to my way of life, now. I'm used to being alone. I have Anita as a companion. I have Andrew as a helper. But I'm cold inside, and I accept coldly that it will be months, perhaps, before I have my family back. All of them. But I intend to do it. I intend to find them. I'm quite determined . . .'

Françoise nodded thoughtfully. 'I know. I can tell. And I'm sure you will. That coldness that you can tell in yourself . . . my God, it's like ice. When you came into the bedroom just a few minutes ago, it was like an Arctic wind blowing into the room.'

Frowning, Brady said, 'A physical cold?'

'Very much so. To my senses only, of course. But I am very frightened of that coldness, Dan. I'm trying to be good. I'm trying not to read you, or to get an insight into you that you would regard as an invasion of your privacy

. . . but with you it's hard not to. Such bitterness. Such quiet, overwhelming anger. Such cold.'

'It'll go,' Brady said. 'When I have Alison in my arms, and Marianna is making *papiér maché* dolls again, and Dominick is setting traps for woodland sprites, and I can't hear myself think because of the arguing . . . it'll go. All of it.'

'I hope so,' Françoise murmured quietly. 'For your sake. And for theirs . . .'

Being Sunday afternoon, the City of London was almost totally deserted. They drove easily through the streets, passed over the flow of the deeply subterranean River Fleet, and thus came into the concreted landscape that covered what had once been the marshy soils bordering the River Walbrook. Thirty years before, excavation in the area between Queen Victoria Street and the tiny road named Walbrook had brought to light the remains of an immense temple, dedicated to the Roman god Mithras. A tourist attraction of great significance, the Mithraeum was only a tiny part of the vast Roman city that still lay untouched, and undisturbed, below the commercial heart of London.

Each time a building was torn down, the archaeologists moved in with their teams and a stop-watch, and rescued what they could from the layers of history below the exposed ground. A year, maybe two, and then whatever had not been discovered was destroyed forever. The foundations of modern buildings went into the bedrock itself. Reinforced concrete was not kind to delicate clay brick and water-preserved wattle.

The new site, which gave signs of being a temple every bit as important as the Roman Mithraeum, lay between the Bank of England and the Guildhall, just off the tiny road known as Ironmonger Lane. The work on the site was proceeding apace, and Sundays were the best days to work, since there were more volunteers available. Haddingham had made contact with Doctor Richard DeVere, who was supervising the excavation and cleared the way for Brady and Françoise. DeVere knew Haddingham well.

153

The only thing that Haddingham *didn't* want DeVere to know was that his precious moon statue had been 'taken' away from him.

Tall wooden hoardings had been erected in front of the fire-ruined building, and as Brady stepped down from his Land-Rover he could hear the sound of distant banging and scraping. A number of cars and trucks were parked, and the roadway outside the shell of the building was dirty with the sort of clay mud that would have been dredged up from the lower levels.

Stooping to enter the small door through the hoardings, Brady found himself emerging into an oddly daylit interior. Most of the innards of the building had been stripped away. Great girders spanned the space between neighbouring buildings, giving extra support. The back of the structure was gone, and the excavation had spread well out into the rear of the grounds. The trench was deep. A tent had been erected at the far end of the old car-park, and most of the exposed deep levels were covered over with glistening polythene.

About forty people were working on the site. Their voices, and the sound of scraping and tapping, was almost deafening.

Walking down a wooden ramp, then along a narrow defile of original earth, Brady led the way to the tent. Françoise followed, her face pale, her mind already reacting to the presence of so much past, and perhaps . . . and perhaps to the stored memory of early, violent ritual.

'It's here . . .' she whispered to Brady, as they hesitated and peered down to an expanse of Roman Wall. 'Not *here*, she added, indicating the brickwork, 'I mean . . . around us. Somewhere close.'

'What is? The rest of the statue?'

'Perhaps. Something powerful. The place is almost screaming . . .'

Without thinking, Brady reached out and took her cold hand. He squeezed and smiled, but before he could let go she had secured a firmer grip, and in this way they walked the final yards to where Richard DeVere was working.

154

For a man in charge of such an important excavation, DeVere was astonishingly young. Or so Brady thought. He placed the man's age at no more than thirty. DeVere had bright ginger hair and spectacles; he wore a beard which, though full, had that straggly, thin look of an adolescent's. Wearing heavy brown cord trousers and a thick green anorak, he walked over to Brady and Françoise and greeted them warmly, but with one of the coldest hands that Brady had ever encountered. He was clutching a clip file, and had the stub of a thin cheroot still between his lips, and he shivered violently inside his clothing.

'Always feel the cold on a site,' he explained with a smile. 'It's the sedentary nature of the work, I suppose.' He showed them what he had been doing, a precise, greatly detailed drawing of a small section of the excavation. 'But you have to take advantage of every minute on a site like this. And it's an important one.' He looked quizzically at Françoise. 'Where did Doctor Haddingham say you came from?'

'I'm helping him in the area of psychic archaeology,' Françoise replied evenly. 'In particular, your statuette.'

'Oh really?' DeVere looked instantly interested, instantly fascinated. 'I'm a great fan of psychic archaeology. It still takes a bit of getting used to, but the success rate is good. We use it a lot. Not here, not on the Walbrook site. I mean at King's College. Everything the PA's give us has to be checked by excavation, but that's the beauty of it. If the psychic touch doesn't work, we waste a day's trench digging. If it *does* work, we save years of searching.'

Françoise smiled. 'Well. That's an enlightened attitude which not everybody shares.'

Richard DeVere knew who she meant. 'Soames. Sour-faced Soames.'

'The very same,' Françoise agreed. 'He almost sabotaged my work with the statue. Almost. But not quite. That's a fascinating piece of sculpture you managed to find.'

DeVere led the way into his tent and opened out two fold-away wooden chairs. 'Fascinating . . .' he breathed, his youthful eyes shining behind his gold frames. 'I sensed it, you know. I felt it. There was something about the statue . . . there's something about the whole site, if you ask me.'

Brady interrupted, 'It's haunted? The site?'

'I'm sure of it. A very eerie feeling when you're working there. But I'm not surprised . . . not after what we've found.' Again he looked at Françoise. 'I take it that's why you're here. To get the psychic *feel* of the place?'

She nodded. 'And to talk to you. We have some questions. Maybe you can help . . .'

DeVere smiled eagerly, looking from one to the other. Brady stared back, aware of every gesture, every glance from the professional historian. On the face of it, DeVere seemed as innocent and as obsessed with his work as any academic. But in Norfolk, in the spring, an archaeological group had turned out to have been anything *but* innocent.

It was no longer in Brady's nature to trust. But he wanted to hear what the man had to say.

DeVere placed a wide cardboard box on the table between them, and opened the top. 'What we seem to have,' he said, 'what we've uncovered, is a shrine –'

Brady's heart missed a beat at the sound of the word.

'– a temple, if you like. It's much smaller than the temple to the Roman god Mithras, over by Queen Victoria Street. On the other hand, it's much, much older. And it isn't Roman. And it isn't to Mithras, or any Roman god, as that statuette should have told you. Let me introduce you to a couple of people . . .'

He reached into the box and brought out two bleached white skulls. They were large, and they had no jawbones. 'May I present Eric and Ernie,' DeVere said with a boyish smile. He turned the two skulls to face each other, and shaking one of them to indicate that it was speaking, he said, 'The man's a fool.'

It took Brady a moment or two to recognise that a Morecombe and Wise joke was being made. He smiled feebly.

'Who, or rather what, are they? Murder victims?'

156

DeVere placed the skulls on the table. He brought more bones from the box, neck bones . . . Brady could see instantly that the vertebrae had been cut by a knife or some other blade.

'Ritual sacrifices,' DeVere agreed. 'Beheaded. Eric and Ernie were the first we found. In all, we've taken one hundred and twenty-three skulls from the site. Men, women, children and animals. Five animals, all horses. All the skulls were apparently in the ash and charcoal zone. They'd been piled up, and later distributed about quite a wide area, while the fire was blazing. Many of them show signs of burning, but a lot seem to have been cut from the body *after* the fire.'

'Are we talking about the Boudiccan fire of AD 61?' Brady asked.

'Actually, it was in AD 60,' DeVere corrected. 'But yes. That's what we're talking about.'

'These were victims of the atrocities, then,' Françoise said. She shuddered violently. 'You are right when you say the place is haunted. It's *very* disturbing.'

'You can feel the ghosts?' De Vere seemed genuinely interested.

Françoise rubbed her hands together, then reached out and picked up one of the skulls. Her thin face was even more drawn, her eyes slightly hooded as she coped with her deep-set feelings of discomfort. After a moment she smiled and placed the skull back on the table. Looking up at DeVere she said, 'I'd like to tell you that his name was Marcus Antonius, or something like that, but the bone is dead. But in the air, here, in the ambience . . . I strongly sense fire. And there is a distant, very distant sound, that is screaming. It's not a long way off in space, just in time, but there is an echo. It's very eerie. I can also . . .' She frowned, staring at Brady, who cocked his head questioningly. But she wasn't looking at him, so much as *through* him. 'A sort of chanting. Women's chanting.'

Now her gaze hardened on Brady. 'It's the same as with the stone.' she said. 'A terrible event. I've seen it from both sides now. Although here it's very weak . . .'

Richard DeVere said, 'But your . . . your talent confirms that there was a massacre here. Do I take that as read?'

Françoise nodded thoughtfully. Then: 'Where was the statue found?'

'Would you like to see?'

'I think it would be good to go there. A part of the statue is missing, isn't that so?'

DeVere agreed. 'Two parts. The head and one leg. You saw the main piece . . .'

Brady stood and led the way from the tent. He looked around at the trenches and open pits, at the huddle of people working in what was, in effect, the soil layer of two thousand years ago. He wondered if DeVere and his workers had a story now, associated with both the shrine and the events of the sixtieth year Anno Domini. Did they have an idea of what had occurred, by whom, and for what reason? Reasons above and beyond the simple fact of the Celtic uprising against the Roman presence in Britain . . .

DeVere led them through the excavation, after first securing hard hats for them. As he followed behind, Brady found himself more than a little bored by the glimpses of Roman brick, of shard layers, of ash layers, of post-holes and water-preserved wattle. The 'ambience' was getting to him too, not the musty, earthy smell of the digging, but the echo of those violent events of centuries before . . . that, and the echo of a cry from the woman he loved.

Alison's face haunted him. He didn't understand why he should start to think of her so powerfully in this of all places, but he did. He became suddenly obsessed with the idea that Alison was in deadly danger . . .

An odd thought. She had been in deadly danger since she had been taken from him, from her home, from her life.

Danger. Threat. His stomach clenched and a cold sweat broke out on his face. He felt dizzy, distracted. The clay-earth sucked at him, its rank smell cloying and choking. The chipping and scraping became a roar of monotonous torture.

158

He stopped.

He slapped his hands to his ears, closed his eyes, stifled the scream that he was longing to emit.

'Alison!' he cried, though the cry was subdued, more audible to himself than to anyone else on the site. 'Alison! O God . . .'

He felt the warmth of tears on his cheeks. All sound had receded. He was alone, in a cold place, distressed beyond measure, haunted by sudden, painful memories.

And then a hand gently touched his face, tugged at his fingers, making him open his eyes, lower his arms and look around.

The woman who stood there was beautiful, tanned, with eyes that were wide and almond-shaped, and understanding and warm . . . She smiled. She touched the tears on his cheeks. Her auburn hair was silky and gentle on his face as she leaned forward and touched her cheek to his.

'It seems that you have a talent after all,' she said.

'Françoise . . .' he murmured, sense coming back, meaning coming back, reality driving away the Otherworld of shadows.

'I walked past it without responding,' she said. Behind her, Richard DeVere was scratching his beard as he watched the scene.

Brady looked down. He was in a wide, circular space. The surrounding bank was heavily labelled with the small identifying tags that were attached to stratifications or buried objects.

'This is where they found the goddess,' Françoise said. 'As you walked over it, you stopped and were affected.' She tapped a delicately manicured finger on his wet nose. 'It's strange how psychic talent can show itself when least expected.'

The terror and grief associated with this particular place in the ancient city had interacted with Brady's own deep-seated sadness to fill him with an unexpected, and very powerful, emotion.

Now Françoise herself tried to 'feel' the past by associating herself strongly with the site.

The first thing she felt was the fire, the same sensation of burning and heat that she had received from the statue. But it was distant. It was a faint hint, faint as the drift of woodsmoke from a bonfire on a still autumn evening. Somewhere among the images of fire were the echoes of human voices, screaming as the life behind those voices died. Again, it was a hint, a distant sound, a far-off rumble of thunder.

Then there was silence. A cold wind on her face. Desolation and emptiness. All the seasons jumbled together, but mostly the wind, and the nearby rush and swirl of water.

Bird song.

Trees clustered about her.

A quiet place, a revered place. A place that echoed with the rustling approach of worshippers –

Stag-horns against the bright sky. Woodland masks above naked human forms. Dogs, straining at the leash, yelping and howling as they were walked around the quiet place.

And then SHE was there. The woman. The female entity. Not one human woman, but many, many at different times. There was the touch of a hand on her lips, her breasts, her belly, her thighs. A sudden explosive sexual release, the running of many hands across her writhing ecstatic body.

Red hair, a waterfall of fiery locks, the press of a woman's lips to hers, and the wonderful joining of bodies, a union performed below a cloudless sky, surrounded by the whispering of full-leaved trees.

And then the sadness – the carrying away – the hilltop, to the north – images that paralleled the earlier visions of watching the burning city, while women stood attendance upon her –

Then silence. Desolation.

Then enclosure. And death. The smell of earth. The striking of blows upon her, and her neck ached, and her left leg ached. She seemed to drown in earth, dirt in her nose, her lungs, her mouth, and . . .

★

Came up gagging and retching! Brady stepped forward and jerked Françoise to her feet, holding her tightly by the shoulder as she gasped and choked. She strained to lean forward, and Brady helped her, but when she retched, nothing came.

Around the site, people stopped digging and stood, watching the source of the sudden commotion. Richard DeVere angrily shouted to them to get on with their work.

'Are you all right?' Brady asked anxiously.

And at last Françoise stopped shaking and gagging, and stood up straight. Her face had broken into a sudden sweat, which mingled with the smeared dirt and clay on her features.

'What happened to me?' she asked with difficulty.

Brady said, 'You were fine. Eyes closed, gently swaying. Then suddenly you flung yourself forward and buried your face in the dirt.'

'I was drowning,' she whispered. 'I was buried in earth. Like the statue. Like the . . .' She glanced at DeVere, then turned away from him and she whispered, for Brady's ears only, 'Like the *entity* in the statue . . .'

'Are you sure you're OK?'

'Yes. I'll be fine. I'd like to sit down.'

They went back to the tent. From the medical box, Richard DeVere produced a bottle of brandy and invited Françoise to take a swig, which she did gladly. DeVere smiled through his wispy ginger beard, watching the Frenchwoman with a mixture of amusement and astonishment.

'So that's how it works,' he said.

'What?'

'Psychic archaeology. Four minutes standing still, then a frantic bout of eating the dirt.'

Françoise smiled with him, then added, 'Worse things have happened to me. Much worse, Much weirder . . .'

'I'd really like to hear about them some time,' DeVere said. He was shaking his head. 'I've never seen anything like it. What visions did you have?'

Françoise took another small sip of the brandy, then sat

back wearily in the hard chair. She began to talk. She told, in as much detail as she could, what she had experienced. She told of the sexual feeling, and the sensation of several women being involved at different times with the statuette, and as she spoke, her words were perceived by Dan Brady, listening intently beside her, but not comprehended . . .

She had said the thing that should have had him running from the site, conscious that Alison's time was almost over; but he had missed it. He sat and listened, and when Françoise was finished he asked Richard DeVere how it all fitted with what the archaeologists were discovering.

It would be half an hour more before Brady grasped the danger . . .

'It seems to fit very well,' DeVere said. 'I've developed an event-sequence for the site that accounts for several things we've found. It's just an hypothesis, of course, but I'm sure it's close . . .'

He adopted the mannerism of a lecturer, sitting back in his hard chair and folding his arms over his chest. 'Let's start at the beginning. The Romans invaded Britain forty-three years after Christ. The local Celtic tribes had huge fortified towns at a number of sites, including St Albans, thirty miles to the north of the Thames, and Colchester, in Essex. But there was no town *on the Thames itself* where London is now. The first point on the river that can be forded is just up river of Blackfriars, just beyond the place where the old River Fleet joins the Thames. OK. The Romans pretty quickly set up a trading and commerce centre at that point. They called it Londinium.

'But I think it's very odd that, at such a crucial river crossing, there was no Celtic town.

'Two possibilities: maybe there *was* a town, a small place guarding the ford. It's hard enough excavating early *Roman* London from beneath the modern city. Wattle and daub would have long since been obliterated.

'Second possibility – and this is the one I favour: there was no town here because this was a *holy* place. A shrine. The temple to the Moon Goddess of the Celts, and perhaps to the female deity of an even earlier people – the so-called Bronze Age settlers who first sailed up the Thames.

'A shrine stood right here, almost where we're sitting. It was close to the Thames, and right next to the River Walbrook. The Walbrook was a wide, meandering river, surrounded by marshy ground and with many subterranean tributaries. It was a holy river. It would have been surrounded by alder and willow, and beech and oak trees. It was a site of tremendous magical power, and a place venerated by the Celtic tribes from all over the country. The place of the Moon Goddess, the guardian mother figure. Sacrifices were made to her. Women – priestesses – attended upon her.

'Then the Romans came. They tore down the holy place when they built their own first city. Then they set up their own temples, including an early one where the Mithraeum now stands, just a few yards from here. In other words, the Romans adopted the veneration, but kicked out the ancient Temple of the Moon.

'The Celtic guardians took their shrine north. There's a very interesting local story in Hertfordshire, a sort of folk tale, which refers to the moon being carried on its willow raft to a cave in the north where it sits and watches its old home, until the sun sends down fires to warm its way back. It's a kiddies' story, but it was written down as early as the ninth century, on a manuscript that is now in the British Museum, of course, but which once belonged to the Abbey at St Albans.

'There must have been a strong sense of outrage in Britain that so holy a shrine was so disgustingly treated. Whenever you read the earliest writings concerning the first century AD, there is a strong feeling that some surge of anger passed across the whole country. Something frustrates the people of tribes as far away as Devon and Wales. You get uprisings, attacks, skirmishes, confrontations. The British were *upset*.'

DeVere smiled, and looked a little apprehensive.

'This is where the *real* speculation comes in. I don't think anybody was quite so upset as the warrior queen of the Norfolk tribes, Boudicca herself! She's the magnificent, flame-haired woman who led a hundred thousand Celts in revolt in AD 60, and sacked Colchester, St Albans and of course . . . London. Her husband was a sort of puppet-king, apparently in control, in fact controlled by the Romans. The one thing Boudicca's king-husband did *not* do was object long and loud to the obliteration of the London shrine.

'He died. Boudicca was flogged and her daughters raped. She used that outrage to amass an army and take revenge on the Roman presence in south-east Britain. But I wonder – did *she* kill her husband? Did she engineer the outrageous treatment of herself and her daughters? Her husband was weak. Only one thing mattered to her: restore the Moon Goddess shrine. She raised an army. She raised more tribesfolk at Colchester when she burned the Roman city there. Then she came to unprotected London. London had no walls. She burned it. She fetched the statue of the goddess from its shrine a few miles north and took it back to its old place by the Walbrook. The priests and priestesses of the area made sacrifices of hundreds of the young and old, the Roman and the Celt. They beheaded them and tossed the heads into the river.

'In a way, from that moment on Boudicca *was* the Moon Goddess. She gained power, determination, arrogance. Power helped her burn St Albans. Arrogance caused her army to be defeated a few days later. No one knows what happened to Boudicca herself. Did she die? Did she kill herself? Or did she return to give her spirit, her power, back to the shrine?

'After the burning of that first London, the Romans bricked in and buried this site. That's clear to see. They feared it. They hated it. But they couldn't touch it. They broke the statue and buried it. For three centuries the spot where we're sitting must have been a haunted and avoided place, its walls marked with warning signs and symbols.

Keep away. Here lives the moon. Beware of the moon. There are ghosts behind this wall. Danger.'

For a few seconds both Brady and Françoise were silent, staring at the youthful archaeologist as he toyed again with one of the skulls from his box. Everything he had said fitted so well with the eerie vision that Françoise had experienced with the stone: the watching, the burning, the sacrificing, the touch of the red-haired figure of Boudicca herself.

Slowly, the uncomfortable thought that had been nagging at Brady began to surface. For a moment he couldn't understand why he was so disturbed . . .

'Are you saying that Boudicca was *possessed* by the deity?'

Putting the skull down, DeVere laughed. 'I'm sure she was possessed. But not *literally* by the deity. I don't believe in demons. But Boudicca is strongly identified with the resurrection myth. I'm sure you know what I mean – the warrior who never dies, only sleeps: like King Arthur waiting to come again and save England. Boudicca sleeps. The Moon Goddess sleeps. One day her spirit will be raised and placed in the body of a new Queen. Folklore . . .' He smiled as he spoke.

Then frowned.

Brady was on his feet, his face a pale mask of alarm.

'Have I said something?' DeVere asked awkwardly.

'Oh my God,' Brady breathed. He looked at Françoise, who was sharing his sudden panic. 'Different ritual, different times, different cultures . . .'

Françoise shook her head. 'I don't follow you.'

'Alison isn't a part of a shrine like the one at Anerley . . . she *is* the shrine. *Her body*. Possessed. She is to be the new vehicle!'

Françoise said, 'Take it easy, Dan. That's a long shot. From what you tell me, Alison isn't exactly six feet of flame-haired iron female.'

'She's strong. She's intelligent. Different times,

Françoise. She *is* a powerful woman. It's what you said: many women at different times. The female entity inhabiting body after body, the *living* form of the goddess.'

DeVere was looking from one to the other of them, his face blank with confusion. 'What's going on?'

Ignoring his question, Brady turned to him and said, 'The Walbrook has subterranean tributaries, you said?'

'That's right. Most of them are now a part of the sewer system, but there are deeper branches –'

'Where does it drain from? Where in the north?'

DeVere frowned and shrugged. 'It has a wide, marshy river area. The river itself drained from all the hills around North London as it is now, from Hampstead to Seven Sisters, as far as I know.'

Brady turned away, his heart racing, his skin cold with the sudden momentous understanding to which he had come.

They had taken their shrine – those ancient priestesses – from the river's edge to the nearby hills that looked down towards that river. From across a sea of foliage, they had watched the burning. They had watched from the top of a hill below which was an underground passage, fashioned from the river tunnel itself. A cramped, damp place, were for a few years the shrine had been kept, waiting for its return.

A hill by the city.

The place of ghosts.

The place where Alison Brady's spirit would be sent to the wind, and her body become the vehicle for this ancient lunar power.

Arachne were here. They had snatched back the statue. Now they were ready to raise the moon . . .

Tonight was the first night of the full moon, and Brady realised that it was the most appropriate night for the transfer of power – the most clichéd of horror scenarios marking the certain death of the woman he still loved so deeply.

'Christ Almighty!' he almost screamed. 'Give me

strength! We've got to find her, Françoise! Tonight . . .
it'll be tonight! I'm sure of it. Those kids . . . the river they
found, we've got to find the river. We've *got* to find those
kids!'

11

In the darkness, Pippa Thompson shuffled about nervously. Her hand suddenly touched Flynn's wrist, and he couldn't help jumping slightly.

'You're as scared as I am,' his sister said, but kept her grip firmly on his arm.

'I'm not scared,' the boy said grimly.

Night had dropped about the cluster of deserted warehouses with all the speed of a black cloak flung across them. One moment they had been crouched in their wide, basement hidey-hole, surrounded by comics, tinned food and the wide chalk circle that Flynn had drawn; the next, the grey light from the grilled window above them had vanished, and a haunting gloom had enveloped them.

'Let's have a candle alight,' Pippa whispered, imploringly.

Flynn fumbled for the matchbox, then lit the wick on a small red candle, placed in the dead centre of the circle. He and his sister huddled round it, watching as its flickering yellow flame cast giant shadows on the cobwebbed walls about them.

'We're safe here,' Flynn said reassuringly. But there was an edgy note in his voice. He stared at the candle. Last night he had refused to light it.

'They ain't gonna see a small light like that,' Pippa said urgently. And added, 'Are they?'

'How do I know? I don't suppose. Anyway, the circle gives us protection, and the charms on the wall will turn the hag away . . .'

The candle-flame made the charcoal symbols writhe, like sentient, two-dimensional animals. Pippa stared at them.

'Bet they didn't help Ritchie . . .'

'Well they can't do any *harm*,' Flynn stated emphatically. 'Now be quiet. We ought to get some sleep soon.'

'It's too early. It's too cold. It's too scary.' Pippa shivered as she spoke. In the gloom, her eyes were bright and wide.

Trog City, this most precious and welcome of havens, turned out, when put to serious use – to be an eerie and unnerving location within which to hide. They had always used it by day, and never later than dusk. Now, the walls themselves seemed to whisper and creak, and outside, in the night, there was movement after movement.

'It's just the wind,' Flynn said.

Even as he said it, there was the sound of a footstep on loose gravel somewhere above them. The sound was repeated, a hesitant, cautious noise. Pippa, without uttering a word, crawled closer to her brother and clung on to him. Flynn quickly reached out and pinched the candle dead. They stared up through the darkness.

'It *can't* get us here . . .' Flynn said quietly, and repeated the words, the desperation in his voice more than a little apparent.

A moment later, light began to spill through the small, thick window above their heads . . .

With dusk still an hour away, Brady and Françoise drove north, through the City. They sped along Upper Street, through Islington and Highbury, and eventually cut across towards Kentish Town.

Brady's whole body was shaking, but his mind was cold and the overwhelming despair of a while ago was now under control. He did not feel embarrassed by his outburst. Françoise, too, shared his idea that Alison – wherever she was – was in deadly and imminent danger.

The underground place that Tip McGeary had stumbled across was the place where Alison's body was probably even *now* being prepared for the ritual of the awakening of the moon. It made Brady sick to think of how little time there might be left.

It had all happened so fast. Taber's death was not yet a day and a half in the past. And yet the time since then seemed filled with anguish, and events, and had somehow stretched out into what seemed like a week or more.

Too fast. Brady had been caught unprepared. Only the chance discovery of the underground river by the kids had given him a chance of rescuing his wife. When salvation rested on such coincidence as this, he was right to be nervous of a successful outcome.

He parked the Land-Rover a few hundred yards from the Thompsons' house, and he and Françoise walked the rest of the way to the back entrance. He had made this same journey only a few hours before, and hoped that in the meantime the Thompsons had not decided to contact the police . . .

A selfish, thoughtless wish, since the safety of their two children might well depend on some police help . . .

But a hope that he harboured anyway.

It took some minutes before Rosamund Thompson cautiously peered through the net curtaining on the back-door window. When she saw who it was she smiled and let the two of them in, closing the door quickly behind them. 'Back so soon? Have you some news?'

Brady hated to disappoint the woman. John Thompson appeared in the doorway to the kitchen, and shook hands. 'I'm sorry,' Brady said, with a shrug and an apologetic smile. 'No news, just some information that makes it imperative I find your boy.'

'In case you'd forgotten,' Thompson said coldly, 'the imperative factor never goes away as far as we're concerned.'

'I'm sorry,' Brady repeated, feeling slightly abashed. 'Of course, that's all that matters. Your children. My wife. We find one, I find the other. Your son holds the key. I *must* know where the river was that he and his friends discovered. Listen, I'd like to play the tape again . . .'

'By all means,' Rosamund said. 'Come upstairs.'

Brady briefly told the Thompsons what he thought was

going on. They didn't fully understand the 'Boudiccan' connection. Too much history in too short a time, too ineptly described by too ignorant a teacher. Brady, for all his talents, was no good at facts, figures and dates.

But they shared with him the urgency, the need, to locate what Death Unit 2000 had so grotesquely described as Trog City.

'Obviously underground,' Françoise said. 'Trog, from troglodyte.'

'A cellar. A basement. An old air-raid shelter; or deserted tube station? Is there anything like that that you know of?'

The Thompsons shook their heads. Rosamund said, 'We know the allotments that they use. And an old patch of waste ground. They used the old house . . . number 61 . . . it was deserted for years before someone bought the shell and did it up again. I don't know of any other deserted houses in the area.'

As they were speaking, Françoise was searching through the pages of the comics that littered Flynn's room. She found nothing.

Then Brady played the tape.

They listened in silence, searched every word for meaning, every breath, every sound . . .

The tape was too short. It ended abruptly. It ended unsatisfyingly. Gerry Cronin, the leader of the group, only referred to the various gang hideouts: Airbase 50, Fort Alpha, the Mutie Wasteland. There was much argument from Pippa, and a stern instruction from Gerry to 'stop talking in the ranks'.

No directions, no hints as to where these hideouts might have been. Nothing. Nothing except . . .

It was Françoise who noticed it. She ran the tape back and played it through again, just a short section . . .

Pippa: *I ain't getting involved with Mutants. Or Robots. Or Strontium Dogs. No Way.*

Ritchie: *We've all got to find out what killed Tip. Anyway, Prospects always stay on look-out duty.*

Gerry: *Stop talking in the ranks and concentrate on this.*

171

*What do we know about what happened to Tip? Trooper
Flynn?*

'Stop the tape,' Françoise said. 'Did you hear it?'

Brady shook his head. He ran the tape back again, and
played it.

Stay on look-out duty.

Stop talking in the ranks.

'There! Did you hear?'

'No!' Brady said, exasperated. He ran the tape back.
Played.

Look-out duty.

(The sound of something tapping against paper.) *Stop
talking in the ranks and concentrate on this . . .*

Françoise said, 'He tapped something before he spoke.
Like a man tapping a map with a stick. Drawing attention
to it . . .'

'A map,' Brady whispered. Again he played the tape.
And now he, too, heard the faint sound, an irritable
gesture by Gerry Cronin. By turning the volume up it
became almost too obvious for words. A paper map was
hanging up beside the boy, and every so often he tapped it
. . . and the paper made a crinkly sound that was suddenly
so very clear . . .

'It's a chance,' he said. 'Where do the Cronins live?'

John Thompson told him, then added. 'I'm coming
with you.'

'I don't think so,' Brady said, and was surprised at the
vehemence of the man's reaction . . . and the violence.
Thompson grabbed him by the lapel and almost jerked
him off his feet. 'Damn you. I said I'm coming!'

Brady eased the man's fingers from him, then tried to
calm him down. 'Listen,' he said. 'There will be police
there. And if you come along with us, it might hamper the
search. We'll have to search the boy's room thoroughly.
Maybe the police have already discovered the map. I don't
know. It's our only chance . . . don't do anything to waste
that chance. Please . . .'

Thompson stood thoughtfully for a moment, his face
still solemn and angry. Rosamund clutched his arm and

nodded. 'The man's right, Johnny. Let them go alone.'

'No,' Thompson said grimly, still staring hard at Brady. 'I want to go to where my boy and my girl are. If you find where they are, Mr Brady, I want to come too. You come back here and fetch me. Is that understood? Is that agreed?'

'Agreed,' Brady said. 'I'll come back for you.'

Grief hung in the air of the Cronins' house like cloying smoke. The news of Ritchie Hughes's death, following so closely on the death of the McGeary boy, had turned anxiety to a sorrow-stricken certainty that their own boy would not be found alive.

Gerry Cronin's parents sat in the darkened lounge of their smart semi-detached house, and watched the silent, flickering screen of the television. No sound surrounded them but the hoarse breathing of Mr Cronin, his voice heavy with years, his life racked with crying.

A policewoman admitted Brady to the house, then used her radio to confirm his credentials. Gerry's father came through and stood, red-eyed and haggard, as Brady explained that he and Françoise would like to check through the boy's room, looking for any clue as to where the gang might have gone that previous afternoon.

Watching the distraught man, Brady felt a strong sense of guilt that he had not released the tape to the police that morning. On the other hand, what more could the police make of the simple record that he had? It had taken Françoise's intuition, and acute hearing, to notice what might be a clue.

Besides, the one thing Brady did *not* want was a police infestation in the area where Alison was held a prisoner.

'What exactly are you looking for?' Mr Cronin asked.

'The Thompsons made funny marks all over Ritchie Hughes' wall. Occult marks, like voodoo.'

Cronin shook his head. 'There's nothing like that up there. I'd know if there was.'

'Nevertheless . . .'

173

He shrugged. 'Help yourself.'

Brady went upstairs with Françoise, though the police-woman followed. The boy had been reported missing by his parents only that morning, although his bed had not been slept in. There was clearly a great deal of irresponsibility working in the Cronin family. The father had knocked on the boy's door at nine o'clock, and when there was no answer had decided that Gerry was in bed, or sulking, and had left him alone. They had not seen their son since lunch-time. It had not occurred to them that this was strange.

Gerry's room was a shrine to affluence, and a cluttered, electronic testimony to the spoiling of the only child. Computers, videos, cassette recorders, sci-fi films *bought* not hired, shelves full of comics, expensive models and high-priced glossy books. Brady began to search cautiously among them. Françoise walked around the room, trying to locate the map by intuition, or at least decide on probable locations for it.

After a few minutes the policewoman left the room. Immediately, their search activity increased in pace.

But Françoise had already decided she knew where the 'secret' map was located.

She walked over to the huge picture of a uniformed, helmeted man called 'Judge Dredd' and, on turning his grim, crudely drawn features to the wall, exposed a high-resolution street map of a part of London.

'Well *done*!' Brady said.

They took the map down. It consisted of several sheets from a large-scale *A to Z* pasted together and taped to the reverse of the poster. It was of the North London area, but there were no marks on it at all that Brady could see, no pencil, no pen, no pins. He located the address where the Cronins had their house, and worked his way out in an expanding spiral, running his finger over the sheets, and trying to spot anything that looked like waste ground, or which might give a clue as to the locations of their hide-aways.

The task was too difficult. Roads and railways were easy

to see, but houses weren't marked, and there was no way of telling where a large, blank area was in fact desolate, or just a collection of gardens.

But suddenly, as he ran his finger over the paper, he felt a depression. By holding the Angle-Poise lamp just so, the slight dents in the map where Gerry had struck it with his pointer could clearly be seen.

'Got it!' Françoise said delightedly, and Brady began to breathe with relief.

There were three such marks, and one was clearly a house. The second was actually labelled on the map as 'allotments'. That didn't sound like 'Troglodyte City', although it fitted well enough with the idea of 'Mutant Wasteland', where Tip McGeary had found the way to an underground river . . .

Try as they might they could find no further markings on the map. Noting the locations of all three pointer marks, they turned Judge Dredd's face to the room again, and took their leave.

It was quite dark now. Brady let the Land-Rover idle for a few moments, headlights off, as he scanned the featureless building that seemed to bar the way ahead. The road ended in the sheer concrete wall. Half the houses that lined the street looked empty.

'Trog City, you think?' John Thompson whispered, leaning forward from the back seat.

'How do we get in?' Françoise asked. 'Put the headlights on again.'

Brady did so. Thompson said, 'The house on the right looks empty. Maybe through there.'

They left the car and walked quickly to the end of the street. Thompson's eyesight proved accurate. Number 17 had no windows, a broken, barred door, and a pile of rubbish with an overwhelming odour in its small front garden. Thompson led the way in through one of the windows.

'No floorboards. Be careful.'

He helped Brady through. Françoise managed on her own, jumping lithely and quickly into the gloom. Brady switched on his flashlight and they picked their way carefully through the shell of the house to the back door.

From the junk-filled garden, a small gap in the side wall showed the way into whatever lay beyond the severe concrete façade. Cautiously peering through, Brady saw a wide expanse of broken concrete and gravel roadway, with tall, deserted warehouses on all sides. Two wrecked Triumph Heralds lay there; from the look of them, they had been there for years.

When all three of them were inside this zone of silent desolation, Thompson called softly for his children. There was no reply, no sound. They split up. Françoise had a small pen-light in her bag. Thompson said that his night vision was so good he didn't *need* a torch.

A minute or so after he had lost sight and sound of the others, Brady suddenly felt a sensation of dread. Were they too late? Had the Hag and her dogs got here first? Would they find only the chewed remains of the two black children?

Feeling slightly sick, Brady stepped into the lee of what looked like an old office block. Empty windows stared at him. His feet crunched on gravel and broken glass.

He heard a distant murmur. A child's voice.

Below his feet he saw a flicker of light – it vanished as soon as he noticed it.

He was standing above a glass grid in the floor, a skylight for some basement room. The glass was too thick to have been broken by vandals or the elements. Too thick to see through.

Nevertheless, he shone his torch down to the basement, trying desperately to see what lay below.

He heard voices. A boy's voice. A girl's voice.

They were chanting.

He listened hard and soon picked up the words, though they meant nothing to him.

'*Ojum zoobos manjooz samedi kanzo . . . ojum zoobos . . .*'

12

Pippa was still crying. She huddled in her father's arms, on the back seat of the Land-Rover, while Flynn sat moodily by the rear window, staring out into the dark night. Pippa's sobbing was as much relief as distress, Brady reckoned. Short though the children's time on the run had been, it was traumatic for the girl in a way that her elder brother did not grasp.

'Are you sure this is it?' Brady asked the lad. He was looking at the advertising hoardings that hid a view of the overground section of the London Underground at this point.

Flynn made an inaudible comment, then spoke more loudly. 'Yeah. This is it.'

'So tell me again,' Brady said, and twisted round in the seat to stare at the boy. 'How do I find the river?'

'Tell the man,' John Thompson said to his son. The boy's silent anger had been getting to him since the emotional reunion at Trog City. The relief at finding his children alive and well had induced tears. Now, the emotion past, he was feeling angry at what the kids had done. Brady could sense an explosion developing and wanted to be well away from the Thompsons before it occurred.

Flynn sighed. Then he hunched forward in his seat. 'You want me to take you there? I will if you want.'

'You *won't* if you want,' his father said angrily. 'Damned if you won't.'

Flynn shrugged, as if to say 'see what I'm up against?'

'OK,' he said. 'First, you go over the wall. You go down the slope and go a way through the tunnel. There's another tunnel to the right. At the end of that is the

Wasteland. You walk through the Wasteland, past an old shed. A bit further on, on the other side of the Zone, is the entrance. It's got three marks on it, right? Like charms. It's hidden behind some thorny bushes.'

Brady stared at the lad. Flynn seemed cool and confident now, his wide eyes bright and shining.

'Did you go inside?'

The boy nodded. 'Sure. Why not?'

'What was there?'

'Some skulls. Dog skulls. Some more markings. And the passage down to the water. That's where the Hag is. And her dogs . . .' The last he spoke in a whisper.

Brady hesitated for a moment . . . just a moment. Then he asked softly, 'And is Gerry Cronin still there?'

Pippa whined, snuggling closer to her father's bosom. Flynn stared at her almost angrily, then looked back at Brady. 'The dogs got him. Ate him. He's still there. What's left of him.'

'O God,' John Thompson breathed, and hugged his daughter closer. 'What *have* you damned kids got up to?'

Françoise asked him, 'Will you be all right for getting home? For walking home?'

'Sure,' Thompson said, 'I'll be fine. You go now, and you be careful, as they say. I didn't know there was anything in this until tonight. Now I know there is. It's bad magic, Mr Brady. Miss Jeury, you remember that too. It's bad magic.'

The Thompsons climbed out of the Land-Rover and began the threequarter-mile walk home. Brady fetched his small pack of protective equipment from the back of the car, then locked the vehicle. He realised, with a shock that was both sudden and short-lived, that he was not wearing his talisman.

'Damn!'

When Françoise asked why he'd sworn he said nothing. The talisman had got him out of trouble on two previous occasions. He felt more than a little naked without it.

And yet . . .

Maybe it didn't matter, now. He was about to find

Alison. He was about to face her captors. Something in him, something that was a part of the hunter that he had become, felt better going to this final confrontation with only the power of his own will, and his own hate, and his own love.

Not for an instant did he doubt that he would be triumphant. Not for a moment did he believe that *anything*, short of a twelve-bore shotgun, could stop him now.

They went over the wall, using a coat to protect themselves from the jagged glass on the top. Dropping onto the steep bank, they picked their way carefully towards the tracks. A train went by, a great glow of light and noise, with hardly a passenger visible within that transient cage of brightness.

When it had gone, Brady led the way cautiously into the tunnel. A few minutes later they emerged into the waste ground and used their torches to ascertain that nothing malevolent was waiting for them there.

'What *is* this place?' Françoise whispered, as Brady's torch flung its beam against steep, sloping brick walls and a tight scrub of small trees and tangled bushes.

'An old railway siding, I think. Cut off and forgotten. There must be miles of such places, hidden away all over London.'

'The Mutie Wasteland,' Françoise said, with a thin smile. 'Let's hope that that was just imagination . . .'

They began to half walk, half run through the cutting, keeping to one side of the brick valley where the ground was drier and the vegetation thinner. Old prams, tins cans, bedsteads, bits of bicycles and a hundred other types of scrap waste testified to this patch of land being less isolated than the children's imaginations had portrayed it.

They found the ruined railway hut and flashed light across the waste ground to the far wall, but all they could see was the featureless dark brick rising high above their heads. Something which sounded like a bus droned past, out of sight of them; a motorbike followed. They were close to a road, but somehow impossibly far away from civilisation.

If Flynn's instructions had been accurate, then the two hunters' search-skills were inadequate. It was more than half an hour before Françoise finally called urgently, 'Dan . . . it's *here*.'

She was standing by a section of the wall where Brady had walked minutes before and seen nothing. He was frustrated and edgy, wondering whether the boy had been leading them on, and feeling the blood in his body about to burst his temples as his panic grew . . .

Now, with Françoise's whispered summons, he felt delight, and a very welcome relief. He raced towards her, dropping the torch and taking a moment to find it again as the beam went off. It wasn't broken.

Françoise was already struggling to open the wooden doorway that lurked so unobtrusively behind its shroud of bush and creeper. Brady flashed his torch over the barrier and saw the faint markings. Unlike the crude and amateurish hex marks in the children's rooms, these marks sent shivers of recognition down his spine; the power in them was evident even to the uninitiated.

Brady reached out and added his strength to Françoise's. The door resisted for a moment, then swung open with a sigh, and an exhalation of air so foul that Françoise cried out and slapped a hand to her nose.

Something else fell out of the space beyond the door. Brady caught it, then stepped quickly back, raising his hands in horror and only just managing to stifle the yell of shock that was about to burst from him.

It was the burned and blackened body of a boy, the arms reaching up stiffly, the empty eyes staring up horribly from the black mask of the face. Gerry Cronin, Brady thought at once. Françoise had made a ritual sign on her body, not the sign of the cross, something else.

'Listen,' she said, as Brady straightened up from the body. He did as he had been bidden, and distantly . . .

Water gurgled.

'The Walbrook,' he whispered. 'This is the place.'

'I know it's the place,' Françoise replied. 'I knew it a few minutes ago. Centuries ago, this part of the hill was

180

covered with woodland. The shrine stood back, almost where we came over the wall. We're walking through a place that was once rock . . . except that a channel, a tunnel, had been cut down to the river. I think I saw it when I was handling the statue. There was a deep natural cleft in the rock . . .'

Shining his torch inside the door, Brady saw that the space beyond had the marks of tools on the wall. If this *had* once been a natural feature, leading from hilltop to underground river, it had been enlarged.

When the railway cutting was being made, a hundred years ago or so, no doubt the engineers had found the crevice. They had blocked it off as dangerous. Brady wondered if they had explored it, and if so, what they had found.

He led the way inside. The passage was low and narrow. He had to stoop almost double as he began to edge down it, towards the sound of the water. He had seen the dog skulls at the top, and now his light beam picked out the etched shapes of heads and symbols on both sides of the tunnel. Françoise slipped and struggled behind him. The smell of protective herbs and the iron and clay paint with which she and Brady had daubed themselves was strong. They had touched it to their hands, faces and feet; a simple protective device against the weakest of elemental powers.

Another protective device was clutched in his right hand: his revolver.

The river was close. The sound of its flowing water was softer here than at the top of the passage, whose amplification had distorted the noise of the tributary. At the end of the tunnel down, the passageway levelled out. Brady shone his torch nervously ahead and realised that they were going to have to rise up blind into whatever chamber lay beyond the turn. He could hear no sound of movement, no voice, no whimpering. Françoise was sensing nothing with her peculiar talents. She just shrugged, and made a face that was an apology.

So at last Brady took the challenge and stooped below

the rock underhang. He found an even narrower passage running more or less levelly. The smell of water and stone was strong. The claustrophobic effect was powerful, and he began to feel very anxious. He was almost on his stomach now, and worming his way forward to the area of pitch darkness ahead.

He hesitated at the lip of what was clearly a low-roofed, naturally formed cavern. His torch beam bounced off a slick, sloping ceiling, from which hung thin streamers of green algae. He edged an inch or two forward again and his head came into the place. A moment later he was all the way in, and straightening up.

The river ran at the edge of the chamber. It was shallow but quite wide, and by it, on the slippery rock, were bits of rag, and rope, and clothing, and candles. The chamber was long. On its walls were stone designs: blind faces; tall, lean figures, their heads cowled; skulls and animal heads; and the sign of the moon.

The place was icily cold. The damp air stung on his face. His breath frosted before him, an eerie cloud in his flickering torch beam. As Françoise wriggled through after him, Brady found the carved niche in the wall where – he was sure – a statuette had once stood. There was a sticky substance in that niche now, and he dabbed a finger on it and shone the torch . . . the stickiness was dark. It might well have been blood.

'She was here . . .' Françoise said, and Brady turned quickly.

'*Was* here?'

'I don't think she's here now,' the Frenchwoman added. She had walked to the water's edge and dipped a finger in. 'God, that's cold.' Picking up some of the rags, she felt them for a moment, then put them down. 'This place is deserted,' she said. 'But there is an echo of terrible misery. The sound of the woman crying is terrible. She was kept here, very cold, very hungry, very frightened.'

Brady looked around, the blood in his body boiling with outrage, driving away the inner cold. 'Bastards . . .' he said. 'Bloody bastards!'

182

Françoise, who could just about stand up straight, although the wet strands of green stuff from the roof dragged at her hair, was running her hands across the walls. She reached the niche and drew back with a sudden gasp of breath, as if something had just bitten her.

Rubbing her hands together and staring at that shallow depression, she said, 'It was there. This place is full of old, old memories. But the sound of the woman is the strongest. She was here recently. So was something else . . . something like a woman, but not a woman. Old and evil, and terribly cold. I can't be sure . . .' She turned away, and added, 'I can't be sure, but I think it was the old part of the statue. The hag.'

'That makes sense. This place was guarded. If it was the place of the new shrine, then it must have been powerful in its own right. But where have they gone? I was so sure she would be here . . .'

And as he said the words, so the enormity of what was happening struck him with a force of despair and hopelessness that brought tears of intense frustration to his eyes. He cried out, throwing his head back and striking his scalp against the rock roof. Françoise reached out a hand to comfort him. The cavern plunged into darkness as he dropped the torch and the light went out.

'I'll never find her!' he said, his voice close to being a wail of defeat.

'You *will* find her, Dan,' Françoise said.

But how could he? He had come here, to this subterranean place, convinced that Alison was to be found in its damp, cold confines. She was not. All the signs had led him here. He had nothing else to go on, no other ideas at all. This *had* to be the place of his final discovery. The hill beside the city, as Anita had murmured. The place of the river. The site of the shrine after it had been banished from London . . .

Where *else* could she have been.

Hopelessness was a shroud around his spirit, and he felt himself sinking.

Françoise stripped away the shroud. She said the thing

that was so obvious; she cast the straw at which he could clutch.

'This place is the secondary place. They'll have taken her to the original shrine, to the place of the first landing. That's where we've got to go now, Dan. Come on . . .'

He hesitated, reluctant to leave the damp prison where Alison had spent so many weeks of her life. It had been his best chance, his best hope, and he had arrived too late. They had taken her away again.

It was almost as if . . .

As if they had known he was coming.

Françoise fumbled for the torch. Water splashed gently in front of them. The despair began to lessen. The river noise seemed to grow in volume, changing its shape. It was as if a fish played there, or something was wading through it . . .

The torch beam came on again. Françoise played it on the river, then cried out with sudden shock, clutching at Brady.

A human shape, water streaming from its ragged white robes, was slowly rising up from the stream. Brady backed away until the rock niche was behind him. Françoise kept the torch on the figure, which seemed to radiate a greyish light of its own.

It was the hag-face female that he had glimpsed in front of his house the day before. Long, lank hair, a grinning skull face, and the withered arms stretched out sideways, the fingers spread and wiggling . . .

On each side of it, the waters bubbled. Two amorphous silvery shapes emerged into the cavern, shifting grey shadows, like whirling clouds of smoke. Within the shapeless fabric, Brady glimpsed the flash of teeth and the occasional blink of large, saucer-wide eyes.

Elementals! Stalkers. Mind creatures capable of terrible acts of strength and destruction.

Brady raised his revolver and let off a shot. The explosion was deafening and the whole cavern screamed with the echo. The bullet struck rock *through* the woman's body. And a moment later something struck at his hand

and sent the pistol skidding back towards the narrow entrance to the place.

Hands grabbed his arms from behind. Françoise, too, was caught. Brady struggled in the grip, twisted round, and saw only a faint silvery glow spreading up the rock face. No visible hands held Françoise either, but neither of them could move.

'What's happening?' she gasped, her face twisted with pain and the effort of trying to break free.

'Elementals. Powerful mind forms.'

'Aren't we protected?'

'Not well enough, it seems.'

The torch was out. All illumination came from the shifting image of the skeletal woman. She seemed to be *holding* the elementals. They thrashed at the leash, making the cold river waters boil.

Tendrils of silver light emerged from the hag then, and snaked towards Brady, wrapping around him, weaving a cold web about his body. He found himself dazzled by light and reflectivity. Things moved before him, but they made no sense. The moonglow was blinding, and the grip on his body was becoming stronger, more damaging.

Then, through the glare, a shape came forward, a tall, animal shape, walking erect. Black and hideous, its face was the lolling-tongued face of a giant dog, the eyes blind, the muzzle drawn open in a rabid smile of glistening teeth. The pink human face below it could be glimpsed through the split in the bottom of the lower jaw.

'We knew you would come,' the dog breathed. 'We've been waiting for you . . .'

'Where's Alison?' Brady gasped.

The dog laughed and echoed his words, mocking him. It came closer. Saliva dripped from its jowels. The stink of decay was pronounced. It lifted a hand and pinched Brady's nostrils closed, inserting the other fingers into his mouth. Brady bit down, but the fingers pried his jaws open again, working deeper into his throat, making him gag . . .

'Troublesome Mr Brady,' the dog said. 'But troublesome no more. Not once your throat and lungs are dangling down below your waist. You've led us a tiresome dance. You've cost us quite dearly. But you've taken our bait like a good little fish. The fetches will leave nothing of either of you to ever trouble us again . . .'

Behind it, the two elementals – the fetches – began to emit unearthly screeches, thrashing in the water as if impatient to get to work on their human prey. Brady remembered the feel of the hands on his neck last Christmas, the terrible choking pain as something totally invisible to him had crushed and twisted his neck bones.

Arachne had been waiting for him. They had set a trap, enticed him to the place from which there could be no escape. He was held, defenceless and unarmed, with both human and unhuman executioners ready to dispatch him.

The fingers in his mouth scraped and gouged at the soft flesh of his throat, trying to get the best grip to tear his jaw away from his head, and his windpipe and lungs from his body. He felt his breath cut off. He was only vaguely aware of Françoise's desperate screaming.

Then the explosion came again, and the whole chamber reverberated and echoed. There was a sound like bone splitting, a dull cracking. The dog loosened its grip upon Brady and stared at him blindly, slowly sinking away. A second shot came and the dog mask flew from the man's head, shattered and twisted. Below it, the male, human face was spurting blood from two holes in the left temple. The eyes had rolled up, the mouth sagged. The man, whoever he was, collapsed to the floor.

Almost immediately, the two elementals were released. Through the dazzling haze of the web that bound him, Brady saw them come rapidly towards him. Where they interacted with the tendrils of energy, there was a silent discharge of light that played – a bizarre St Elmo's fire – about the fabric of the mind-created creatures. Brady glimpsed great shoulders and sunken heads, with mouths that gaped wide, and eyes that blinked from beneath heavy folds of flesh and muscle on the brows.

One of them reached for him, claws opening out, five curved knives of ivory.

Then flame seared through the web and something like a whirlwind sucked the silvery tendrils away from Brady and Françoise, at the same time driving back the elementals. Brady thought he glimpsed the towering figure of a nude and black-skinned man standing at the water's edge, a spear rammed through his belly, the point gleaming and glistening with blood. The cavern echoed to several screeched, alien words, and the hag curled up and vanished. All the light in the cavern disappeared. Something thrashed about in the water, then the river was still.

Françoise was breathing hard in the total darkness. She reached out and took Brady's hand. 'What happened?' she whispered.

'I don't know . . .'

There was a movement from towards the entrance. A match flared.

John Thompson stood there, clutching a book in one hand. He was dressed in a white suit, with no shoes and no shirt. He was smiling at them.

'I warned you,' he said. 'But I didn't think you'd listen.'

They crawled back up the tunnel to the outside world again. As they stood in the cold night, below the cloud-covered sky but able to see slightly by the glow of the full moon, Thompson passed Brady's revolver back to him.

'Was that a man or a dog I shot?'

'A man wearing a mask made out of a real dog's head. It's one of the trademarks of Arachne.'

'Sounds smelly,' Thompson observed, shivering slightly and clutching the leather-bound volume he held a little closer to his chest. He asked, 'Your wife wasn't there, I take it?'

Brady shook his head, still confused by what had happened, still shaken. 'They were expecting me. They'd set a trap. They knew I'd be looking for her, so they made it easy for me.' He laughed sourly. 'Only I made it difficult for myself. I found out where they'd been keeping Alison by tracking down two kids who'd stumbled on the place by mistake. If I'd stayed at home they would have let me know anyway. They wanted me here. They thought they could destroy me because I'd be expecting to fight for Alison, and not defend myself . . .'

Thompson smiled. 'They damn near managed it.'

Brady said, 'They *did* manage it. What the hell happened down there? I have no right to be alive now. Nor Françoise . . .'

Thompson raised the book. 'I couldn't use this to find my kids; you found them for me. I'm grateful for that. I promised I'd never use the *hunganzi* for any purpose except the people's purpose. My people, not your people. But then I thought, what the hell? You looked naked to me. And I figured I owed you one. So I followed you here as soon as Errol and Pippa were safely spanked and in bed.'

Françoise reached out to touch the book, then jerked her hand back. Thompson smiled at her, a knowing smile, then winked. She said, 'I saw a naked man. He had a spear in his stomach. Was that you?'

Thompson laughed out loud. 'Hell no. And I hope it never will be.'

'You used Flynn's little charm, then. The spell to turn around a hag . . .'

Thompson shook his head. 'There ain't no spell. Not as such. Errol thought like you do. That the *hunganzi* is a spell book. He copied the charms out. But that's silly. They ain't charms. They're tattooes. You ain't even supposed to *look* at them. To use the *hunganzi* you use the whole page. You tear it out, screw it up and throw it. That's what I did.'

'Where did the man come from.'

Looking at Françoise, Thompson waved the book. '*This* is the man. What you saw was the spirit of the man. A powerful spirit because of what was done to him.' Looking back at Brady, he waved the book again. '*This* is the man. It's not a book. His name was Jacob Matthews. To make a *hunganzi* you kill the man with a stone-tipped spear. Then

188

you crush the body and spear until it's just a soup. Blood, bones, skin and brains. All crushed in a big stone vat like wheat grains in a quern. Then it's mixed with clay and fibre, and rolled out to make parchment. Each sheet has a different spell. When all the sheets are used up, the spirit of the man is released.

'*Hunganzi*. The blood book. The man book. It's a magic more powerful than voodoo . . .' He opened the sheaf of parchment pages and tore one out. 'And it's yours. Or part of it . . .' He passed the sheet to Brady.

Brady took it. It felt unpleasant to the touch, like an old man's skin, wrinkled and dry . . . yet somehow living.

'What spell is this?'

Thompson said, 'It'll counteract moon madness. From what you tell me, the moon is your enemy tonight. That'll stop the moon. What else might you need?'

'Protection against dogs?' Brady suggested, and Thompson nodded, removing another sheet from the book. Then he passed over a black linen cloth. 'Don't look at what's written on them. Just ball them up and throw them. *Hunganzi* will do the rest.'

Brady folded the sheets into the linen and tucked them into his small pack. He shook hands with Thompson.

'I'm indebted to you.'

'We both are,' Françoise said.

13

She had cried for an hour, and despite Haddingham's best efforts to interrupt this expression of Anita Herbert's shock, he could not break through the flow of tears.

When she finally stopped sobbing she fell asleep. She slept until darkfall, a deep, peaceful slumber; her breath still rattled in her throat, but she no longer looked in pain, and the greyish hue of her face had vanished. Her cheeks were rosy again.

Haddingham sat downstairs, moodily staring at the empty fire grate and thinking muddled thoughts. He was on the point of going to the kitchen to rummage around for some supper when he heard the girl call out from upstairs.

She was sitting up in the bed, looking sleepy and confused. She frowned when Haddingham came in. She knew him vaguely, having met him briefly on two occasions.

'How are you feeling?' he asked.

Anita touched her throat gingerly. 'Terrible,' she said, her voice a hoarse croak. 'Where's Dan?'

Haddingham went over to sit on the bed. 'He's left me in charge of you. You gave me quite a start a few hours ago. I thought you'd come round, but you went into shock.'

She nodded, as if she remembered the event. 'I saw Alison . . .' she said. 'She was outside, calling to me. I went out into the field and . . . and she changed. Horrible . . .'

Suddenly she turned frightened eyes on Haddingham. 'Where *is* Dan?' she asked again, becoming agitated.

'He's in London. Looking for Alison. He's gone to fetch her.'

190

To his surprise, Anita immediately started to struggle out of bed. 'Oh no!' she cried. 'He mustn't. I've got to go after him . . . '

Haddingham restrained her gently. 'Take it easy. You're not well enough to go gallivanting up to the city. He's safe enough. He thinks he knows where she is . . .'

'Let me go!' Anita insisted and an edge of real panic crept into her voice.' It's a trap. Don't you understand?'

'A trap?' Still Andrew held her back.

'They're waiting for him,' she said. 'It's a trap. They know he's coming. We've got to stop him!'

Her words were like icy blows. A trap? Expecting him? Anita struggled out of bed and stood, shakily, in just her underclothes. As she reached for her jeans, her knees buckled and she went down on the floor. Haddingham helped her up and put her back in the bed. She was shaking like a leaf.

'You're too weak,' he repeated. 'Keep calm. We'll do something. First: how do you know?'

'I heard her say it . . .' Anita said, miserably.

'Heard who say it?'

'The old woman. A horrible corpse of a woman. She's the one who . . .' – touching her throat – 'who strangled me. They tricked me out of the house and tried to kill me. I saw a funny vision. This house went away and there was a much older building in its place. Like a Roman villa. And there were hundreds of men riding past it. They killed the people who lived there, and a woman carried one of the heads and impaled it on a spear. There was no mistaking her. Tall, red-haired, a queen in a small chariot. She could have stepped right out of the history books.'

'Boadicea?'

'Boudicca. None other. It was *horrible*. What they *did* to those people . . .'

Haddingham was thinking of the vision that Françoise Jeury had had, a similar sight of a flame-haired woman.

And you heard her say they were waiting for Dan . . .'

'I'm sure of it,' Anita said huskily. 'Alison is on the hill by the city, the old place of ghosts . . .'

'That's where Dan has gone. To the hills to the north of the old city. Highgate, Hampstead, that sort of area . . .'

But Anita was shaking her head. 'I don't think that's right. The hill *by* the city. They've set a trap for him in the north, to kill him. We've *got* to warn him . . .' Her voice cracked with desperation, and she rubbed her throat, trying to soothe the discomfort.

'The hill by the city . . .' Haddingham repeated. He shook his head. 'Wait in bed. Don't try and get up. Please . . .'

'I won't. Just *do* something.'

Haddingham ran downstairs quickly and went into the small room that had once served both as study and library. Two walls were covered with books and journals, and he scanned them furiously. 'Come on . . . come on . . . there must be *something* here . . .'

After about five minutes he noticed a book on the top shelf: *Reconstructing the Past*. He reached up and plucked it down, and saw to his delight that it consisted of paintings, reconstructions, of the old Roman and Saxon towns of England.

There was a whole chapter devoted to London, and although the paintings were dark and badly reproduced, the text contained what he wanted . . .

He read quickly. To the east of the city were two small hillocks, where now stood the Tower of London and the Mint. To the west, a single hillock marked the edge of the city.

And on the hill . . .

'Good God,' Haddingham said. 'Good God Almighty . . .'

He slammed the book shut and ran through into the lounge, quickly leafing through a telephone directory. He snatched the phone from its cradle and began to dial a number.

Half-way through, he stopped.

If he alerted them, it might prove Alison's undoing. If he phoned the warning through, it might jeopardise Brady's chances of rescuing his wife.

Damn and double damn. What should he do?

He had to find Dan Brady. That meant either contacting Andrew Sutherland, or trying to pin him down through Richard DeVere at the Walbrook excavation. DeVere was contactable by radio telephone.

Haddingham dialled again.

It was after ten o'clock as Brady drove like a madman, back into the bleak concrete jungle that was the City of London. The streets were deserted, eerily lit by neon lamps, which cast great grey shadows against the featureless expanses of white and grey brick. On all sides, walls rose sheer and claustrophobic, small dark windows, reflecting the headlights of the Land-Rover as it veered and screeched round corners.

There was not a single, solitary human form to be seen. Not even a policeman.

As he leapt from the vehicle, across the road from the entrance to the Walbrook excavation, Brady shivered with the sudden blast of icy cold. A desperate wind blew through the concrete channels that formed the City streets. It penetrated his windcheater, froze him to the marrow. The night was dark, cold and cloudy, and Françoise, too, felt the diminishing of her spirit.

Still badly shaken by the experience in the river cave in North London, she followed Brady into the burned-out shell of the Ironmonger Lane building.

They approached cautiously, keeping to the shadows. About twenty people were still working on the site. There were four floodlights, casting a dazzling glare across a small part of the excavation. The murmur of voices and laughter seemed quite normal.

Brady watched the scene, and his despair grew. Two girls in thick anoraks carried something bulky and dirty out of a trench and up towards the tent where, earlier, DeVere had entertained them. A bearded young man slipped on mud, and laughed as he was caught by two friends. He swore and brushed at himself, and Brady heard someone say. 'That's a hundred and fifty years of Roman London crushed by one bloody great boot.'

Someone called, 'Does the ash layer go *above* the orange silt, or what? It's all fucked up over here.'

'Above,' came the reply.

'Anybody making tea?' called a girl's voice. 'I'm gasping.'

It was all too normal for words. There was nothing supernatural occurring here. Brady stared at the crouched figures, at the glaring lights, at the scudding clouds that covered the moon, and thought, *so this is how it ends. I had my chance, and I blew it. I'll never find her now. Never. Never!*

'Never . . .?' said Françoise, frowning. 'What do you mean 'never'?'

'Was I talking aloud?' Brady asked. He shrugged. 'She's not here. Let's face it, there's nothing happening here. What the hell do I do, Françoise?'

'I don't know,' she said quietly. Then she stepped forward, further into the site, and crouched on the ground above one of the trenches. She spoke to two of the students for a moment, then came back to Brady.

'DeVere has gone home. Apparently, Andrew called him earlier. He's left a message that if you *should* come back, could you call him urgently.'

Brady shuddered. 'Anita, do you think?'

'Maybe. You want to find a phone-box?'

Brady stared at the working group, then nodded. 'Yes. I suppose I should. Damn!'

His sudden expletive was a mere gesture of fear and frustration. He turned back from the site and walked to the Land-Rover his fists balled, his teeth clenched to try and stop the scream of anxiety from emerging. 'What do I *do*?' he said to no one in particular. 'What in God's name do I do?'

'Let's drive,' Françoise suggested. 'Maybe we'll see something.'

They climbed into the Land-Rover. Brady sat silently for a moment, then switched on the engine and almost skidded as he streaked away from Ironmonger Lane.

They drove for twenty minutes. He went as far north as Clerkenwell Road, then came zig-zagging back down Farringdon Road and Charterhouse. He went round Smithfield, then down past the Old Bailey to Ludgate Hill. He drove round St Paul's Cathedral, along Cannon Street, and back towards the Bank and the silent, empty streets again. Then, with the tears rolling down his grey, cold cheeks, he swung the vehicle about, and drove back to the river, speeding across Southwark Bridge and parking almost dead centre, above the wide, silent flow of the Thames.

He got out of the car, drew his jacket tight about his throat, and went and leaned morosely against the iron rail at the side of the bridge. Françoise joined him and linked her arm through his. They stood there in silence and stared at the lights of the city, and the majestic skyline formed by its buildings, both ancient and modern.

'So close . . .' he said disconsolately, and kept repeating the words. 'So close . . . so close . . .'

There was nothing that Françoise could say for a while. Then:

'Let's go and ring Andrew. Come on, Dan. The game's not over yet . . .'

Brady hesitated, then nodded and straightened up. 'Yeah. Perhaps you're right.'

He turned away from the river, reaching into his pocket for the keys to the Land-Rover . . .

And stopped.

Françoise had stopped too. They were both staring towards the City, both frowning, both uncertain as to what exactly they were witnessing.

The dark clouds were a bright, silvery grey where the full moon was trying to peer through to the streets below. The bright skyglow was a very natural sight, but somehow, now, it seemed stronger . . . stranger . . .

The glow was above the great dome of St Paul's. As they watched, so a silver strike of light leapt down from clouds to cathedral. Françoise gasped as she witnessed it. A second tendril of moonglow played on the gleaming dome, and then was gone.

It was as quick as that.

For a second, the two of them just stood and stared. Then Brady remembered the earlier drive – *up* Ludgate Hill and round the cathedral.

St Paul's stood on a *hill*.

A hill by the city. A place that must have been a religious place for thousands of years.

St Paul's!

Without a word, both of them jumped back into the Land-Rover and Brady began to drive to save a life!

In the dark place, among the silent tombs of the dead, the moon began to return to the stone, and the spirit of *Aipeona* stirred.

Time meant nothing to the entity. That it had been trapped here for nearly two thousand years did not concern it. She was the female spirit of earth and moon, and she had slept and dreamed of what had been, and now the moonglow was returning, and there was a new life, a new release . . .

New power.

Aipeona. Moon Goddess. White Goddess . . .

Ancient. And hungry . . . And eager to exert her power in the mortal world again. As the moon brought strength and feeling back to her, as the stone warmed, as the crystals buzzed and hummed with life again, so she could sense the strong, young body that she would soon inhabit. Tall. Slim. Athletic . . . Sexual. She tasted the sweat, ran a probing tongue across the sweet flesh, felt the fear in the woman, and the experience, and the passion . . . longed to take her. Longed to possess her.

This mortal . . .

This vessel . . .

This beautiful body called Alison . . .

★

196

In the darkness, the woman Alison watched the broken stone with growing fear. It was the first time, since she had been moved from the warm house to the cold, damp river cave, that she had been more than distantly aware. The past was an unreal blur to her. She had images in her mind of Christmas, and of darkness. She remembered being tied and carried through a long, cold night. There had been a caravan, and her daughter – and the despair of not knowing what had happened to her son and her husband. Then there had been a house which smelled, and a cellar with bats. And sleeping, always sleeping. Her dreams were full of images of moving about, through strange countryside, then locked in bleak houses, then in cars and moving, then in damp places . . .

And always so lonely.

At last there had been the river cave. And now, here, this place of tombs.

Her breathing was gentle, but anxiety made her breath harder. Her arms were tied behind her back. She was kneeling.

As the drugs continued to wear off, she looked around. It was a small, hesitant movement. She was aware that she was naked, but for a thin, knee-length shift. Cold metal bracelets were around her ankles and her wrists; something cold and heavy was dangling round her neck.

In the silent crypt, things stirred. She watched the stone in the darkness, aware that it was glowing faintly. The hag's head grinned at her, watching her. The child's face in the belly was blinking awake. The statue was standing, apparently unsupported, on its single intact leg.

Where am I? What's happening? How long have I been . . . ?

Then a tendril of silvery fire snaked down from above her and played gently on the stone.

It vanished as quickly as it had come, but immediately the light emanating from the figurine of the woman began to increase in intensity. It spread out into the tombplace, and a shadowy gloom replaced the blackness.

She saw that she crouched in a semicircle of eight

human shapes. Each of them was kneeling, with its head drooped and its arms stretched out to the side. They were all quite motionless.

Two of them, the two in the centre of the half-circle, were women, wearing black robes. The others were men. There was something strange about the men's heads, something unhuman . . .

The brightness from the stone suddenly increased dramatically and the whole crypt filled with the hissing of breath being drawn. Heads came up and the eight figures stood in quick, strangely smooth motions, as if a film of their kneeling down had been suddenly reversed. Their arms lowered, their bright eyes turned to stare at the woman who watched with growing alarm.

The sunken, shrivelled features of the two hags grinned at her. The dead faces of horses stared at her from the others. The crypt began to fill with an eerie whispering noise, and she could sense words, strange words, and the name *Aipeona*, repeated almost urgently.

From the small stone statue a writhing snake of silver fire began to worm towards her . . .

The great cathedral was in darkness, the last Christian service long since finished. Floodlights played on it, illuminating the round windows, the great rise of its walls, the immense dome. But St Paul's seemed dead, silent, a solitary monolith on the hill, set apart from the surrounding buildings.

Brady ran across the plaza in front of the church, and up the wide stone steps. He moved along the row of heavy wooden doors, trying them all. They were locked, of course. He banged his fist against one of them in frustration, and would have repeated the blow had not Françoise restrained him.

'We'll have to jimmy the door open,' he said.

'And set off the alarms? What good would *that* do?'

She was right. Brady trotted back down the steps, wary for a police patrol car and conscious that the streets around

198

St Paul's were not totally deserted. Cars drove noisily past, and a few pedestrians moved quickly through the shadows. He looked up at the building. 'There's *got* to be a way in. You take the north side, I'll take the south . . .'

They split up and ran quickly round the cathedral. Some of the windows were quite low. The beautiful stained glass caught stray light from the street-lamps. It would be sacrilege to break in through such a work of art, but if it came to the choice between that art and Alison's life . . .

He expected to meet Françoise at the back of the cathedral, but she wasn't there. He ran quickly round to the north side, a narrow street between the church and a row of law offices.

Françoise was standing there, beckoning to him. She was at the top of a narrow flight of steps that led down to the passage to the crypt. At the entrance to that passage was a metal grill. She gently moved it, and it folded up on itself.

The lock had been forced.

They stepped into the passage, into the darkness.

After a few yards, more steps went down into the earth, passing through the foundation walls of the huge building. Françoise used her small pen-light to show the way. Brady held his revolver in one hand, and the unwrapped parchment pages of the man-book in the other.

Steps went up, and at the top of them: a heavy oak door. Françoise opened it as quietly as possible.

Silver light spilled from the cavernous chamber beyond.

They were in the crypt. Ahead of them, Nelson's tomb was a prominent and proud monument. The ceiling was high, supported by thick round pillars. The vault was vast, but divided into alcoves, secret places, with steps rising up into gloomy little niches where the famous dead of ages were entombed.

There was an odd scent in the place, like burning tallow. But more pronounced was the smell of fresh earth.

And the whole place whispered.

Edging slowly between the tombs, Brady approached the source of the silver glow. The whispering got louder.

He could make out words, but they were in no language that he understood. He could also hear the terrified whimpering of a woman. Françoise reached out and quickly squeezed his hand. Brady glanced at her. By the strange light her face looked grey and drawn. She knew the danger. She was frightened. Yet she had followed him into this situation without being asked, without making conditions. She had perhaps not even *thought* about the possibility of abandoning him.

Warmed by the thought of how committed Françoise was to helping him, Brady took another step forward, coming round a pillar and looking to the small side alcove from which the light was coming.

He almost died.

The ring of figures, with their horse-head masks, was terrifying enough. But he had eyes for two things only. Alison, kneeling, her back to him. Alison – his lovely Alison – he recognised her at once, her hair, the shape of her shoulders . . . Her hands were behind her, tied with silver chains . . .

Towering above her was a glowing female shape. It was immense; its head was bowed slightly, but still it touched the high stone ceiling of the vault. Its breasts were huge, its belly swollen, its thighs like great slabs of pale marble. Its hands were on Alison's face, cradling her head, moving the head from side to side. The gigantic naked shape moved in slow motion. Its hair drifted about its shoulders like seaweed in shallow water. Its mouth was opened wide and the tongue licked out, a snake, tasting the air.

Huge eyes glowed moon bright. The eyes were slanted, elfin . . . evil.

As Brady watched, so this hideous creature opened its mouth even wider and stooped down to take Alison's head between its lips.

'No!' Brady screamed. He raised the revolver and shot at the towering spectre. The bullet impacted with one of the horse-masked figures behind, flinging it backwards. Françoise snatched the *hunganzi* sheets from him and took one out, crushing it in her hand –

Movement towards them.

Alison struggled, as if suddenly coming to consciousness. She turned round as she knelt, and saw her husband. Her pale, drawn face registered a sudden overwhelming joy. 'Dan! O God. Dan! Quickly!'

The lips touched her head and she screamed.

Françoise flung the *hunganzi*. Fire exploded, a great expanding ball of red flame in the middle of which appeared the naked shape of the man whose body was the fabric of the book. The female entity straightened up and screeched, stepping heavily back. The horse-masks retreated. The hags shrivelled up, crouching down, raising their arms to protect themselves from the flames.

Brady ran through that cold fire and grabbed Alison. She struggled to her feet, but her legs went out from under her, and Brady dragged her across the marble floor as she sobbed with both relief and terror.

The flame played on their skin but didn't burn.

'Dan! Watch out!'

Françoise's cry of warning made Brady duck, even as he was frantically looking around to see where the danger lay. Something passed close to his neck, and he glimpsed the shaft of a spear as it clattered against a pillar. He looked up quickly as he heard a horse whinny in complaint.

The animal was rearing up onto its hind legs. It was attached to a small wicker chariot. A tall woman stood in the chariot, her arm raised as she prepared to throw a second spear. Flame-red hair drifted about her head and shoulders, but the face that watched Brady was the sunken, evil mask of a corpse.

Françoise flung the second *hunganzi* sheet. The horse screeched and reared again, pawing the air as the ghostly man-figure grew from the parchment, hands raised, a yellow fog swirling around his body. The spear that had killed him glistened red in his belly. The chariot swung round as the phantom horse panicked. Ghost versus ghost, the Celtic magic disturbed by this unfamiliar supernatural counter.

Brady flung Alison's inert body over his shoulder and

ran with her, back towards the entrance to the crypt. Françoise followed, then led them along the dark passageway and up to the street.

The street was deserted and silent. Lamplight filled the air with a yellow glow. The moon was behind dark clouds, but the area around the sombre, towering edifice of St Pauls basked in the artificial light, an eerie and false brightness in this dead time of night.

Silence. Brady looked around, orientating himself . . .

There was a sound like a box lid creaking open. The pavement below their feet trembled and shook. Glass shattered somewhere. A horse complained and a woman shouted, her voice shrill and angry . . .

A moment later, the horse and chariot with its terrifying occupant seemed almost to burst up from the ground, turning sideways on to the cowering group as the skull-faced warrior queen looked from one to the other of them. Then she jerked at the reins, raised a spear and the horse began to run, the iron-rimmed wheels of the chariot rattling on the paving stones.

Brady ran for his life, Alison's weight dragging him down. Françoise kept hold of his hand, pulling him forward as they raced down the narrow street to the back of the cathedral.

The ghostly woman screamed. The chariot bore down on them. Turning as he ran, Brady saw the woman's hair and cloak spread out on the wind, great flowing wings of fire.

The Land-Rover was a long way away. Brady had no idea where to go.

And then there was movement ahead of him, a figure stepping from the shadows between two kiosks.

'Over here, Dan!'

It was Andrew Haddingham! Where in God's name had *he* come from?

'Quickly, Dan!'

Haddingham was running towards him. For all the world he looked like a City businessman, in dark suit and tie. His car was parked close by. The chariot, though, was even closer, clattering in pursuit, the woman rider screaming in her alien tongue.

Haddingham flung something beyond Brady and Françoise. Brady glimpsed a small, dark object. It rattled on the ground in front of the spectral horse.

The chariot turned side on. The spear was thrown, but as it whistled through the air, so it vanished. The horse and chariot twisted and turned, the corpse-face watching them almost angrily, but the whole phantom seemingly unable to move forward.

'Come on!'

Haddingham took Alison from Brady's shoulders and carried her to the car. They bundled inside, Brady in the back, with the weeping woman for whom he had been searching for nearly a year. He held her hand so tightly that, even as she cried, she was trying to loosen the grip; but Brady wasn't ever going to let her go again.

'What did you throw?' Françoise asked, and Haddingham grunted. 'A small Roman statue – borrowed, I'm afraid. One of their gods. Mithras . . .'

'No Celt would like that,' Françoise agreed.

Haddingham laughed as he started up the motor. 'Thank God we're dealing with superstitious people.'

In the back seat, Alison stopped weeping. She looked at Brady. He looked back at her.

'O *God* I've missed you,' he said.

Her eyes screwed up and tears came. She flung herself into his arms and hugged him so tightly that he thought she might dislocate his neck.

After a few moments he smiled, and let his own tears of joy flow freely.

EPILOGUE

From the dining-room window, Andrew Haddingham watched Dan and Alison Brady as they walked, arms around each other, through the apple trees, down towards the uncovered remains of the Roman villa. It was late morning. Alison had slept until eleven. Brady had sat by the bed all night, staring at her. Just staring.

Françoise Jeury had returned to London, taking Anita Herbert with her. The girl was confused and upset; for a while, at least, Haddingham thought it would be best if she was not around. What she had done was very well appreciated, and her support for Brady was not yet finished.

The police had been and gone, leaving only the MoD man to look after the reunited couple. Nothing had been found in St Paul's, apart from the damage. No bodies, no statue – nothing except the small statue of Mithras which Haddingham had so prudently procured and used. No sign of Arachne had been found in the river cave either, though Gerry Cronin's body had still been there, completing the tragedy of the families of Death Unit 2000.

That Arachne had laid a trap for Brady was not in question. The witch-guardian of the moon shrine had come to Brook's Corner to entice him to that trap, and finding him absent had tried to destroy something it imagined he loved: Anita. Meanwhile, Brady had been carefully, and unwittingly, guiding himself into the very trap they had laid for him.

When Haddingham had intuited the St Paul's connection he rushed to the archaeological dig, then to the cathedral – which was full of light and sound and song – then to a colleague in Kensington from whose collection of reputedly 'haunted' artefacts he borrowed the Mithraic totem. Brady's Land-Rover was by the cathedral on his return, and as he searched for his friend and colleague, so the fleeing man burst into his field of vision, Alison's body slung across his shoulder.

The most unsatisfactory part of the whole intense and complex affair was the abandonment of such a source of power in their panic at getting Alison back to safety. At least seven of Arachne's growing élite had been in the crypt of the church, and made good their escape with the statue of the Moon Goddess.

For them, for that small but significant part of the purpose, there would be another day, another ceremony . . .

Another life to play with.

As the Bradys disappeared from sight, Haddingham smiled and turned away from the window. For the moment, worries about Arachne seemed a long way away. There would be an hour, perhaps a few hours, during which the two people would have nothing on their minds but what their *own* future held for them. The love, the support, the starting over. And of course . . .

Their children. Marianna. Dominick. Still lost . . .

It was cold outside. Alison was shivering slightly and she snuggled closer to Brady.

'Tell me this isn't a dream,' she said quietly.

'You tell *me* it isn't,' he said back, and squeezed her tightly, his eyes closing with the pure and simple ecstasy of the feel of her, of the certainty of her reality. 'Christ! I've missed you so much!'

'It all looks so different here,' Alison murmured. 'Everything is different . . . and I don't want it to be . . .' She shuddered, then turned tear-filled, angry eyes on Brady. 'I want it to be exactly as it was. No different. I want the four of us as we were. No ghosts, no defences, no fear of the dark . . .' Her shaking grew violent, and the tears came again, her hands clutching at his clothes desperately.

Considering what she had been through, she was

remarkably composed, coping unbelievably well. But Françoise had detected the great storm of despair and terror that was lurking deep within her. It would have the effect of a terrible explosion of shock. The family doctor, who had visited early in the morning, had agreed. Alison was fit, if very thin, and not obviously ill in any physical way. The concern of all around her, all who loved her, was to what extent she was harmed in the mind – and how would that harm show? And how self-destructive might it be?

For most of the months of her captivity she seemed to have been in a dazed state of semi-consciousness. The events of the Christmas night were vivid to her, in the way the scenes in frightening films were vivid – they shook her, but were somehow remote from her. She remembered being moved a lot. She remembered houses with smelly rooms. She remembered the voices of men, and the soothing voice of a woman. There was pain in these memories, but also darkness.

Not until the sequence of captivity in the dark, damp cavern below North London had she found herself fully conscious again . . . to her, at that time, only a few days seemed to have passed.

It frightened her more than anything to discover that nearly ten months had gone by since her family had been attacked.

For Alison, then, there would soon be a gruelling return to the true reality of her existence. While her mind and her body made that slow and painful journey, Brady would be there to help, beside her, his arms around her. There would be hypnosis, to unlock the sights and sounds that she had accumulated but now forgotten: there would be questions: there would be a forcible reliving of the events that had begun her personal nightmare.

And yet . . .

If Brady had resolved to spare her the worst part of the situation for the moment, to give her the full details of the evil and the power which they were up against at a later time, he had reckoned without the strength and the

206

endurance of the woman whom he had married. Alison knew full well that her two children had been taken from her. She remembered the night, the blackness, the cowled shapes, the screaming ... She remembered a few moments, in some bleak room, when she and Marianna had hugged each other in terror, and watched as something that was a cross between a man and a pig prowled about that room, its breath a ghastly hissing sound in the grey light.

She remembered waking and finding Marianna gone, and the loneliness had been intolerable for a while, before the drugs had reduced her mind to a twilight zone of soft sound and timelessness.

And now, in the garden, bitter hate and a terrible anger stirred in her pale, thin breast. She walked away from Brady, climbed up onto the wall around the garden, and peered into the distance, to the woods where Anita had almost lost her life.

'I want my children *back*!' she shouted. '*Do you hear me? I want my children* back!'

And she repeated the cry, again and again and again, her voice rising in pitch, expanding in volume, her hands clenching, her body becoming a rigid column of bone and muscle. 'My children ... my children ... my children ...'

Soon the sound was a repetitive shrill of hysterical passion. The words and the sentiment were a chilling symphony of determination and fury.

She stopped quite suddenly. She coughed, then rubbed her eyes and her arms. She stepped down from the wall and came up close to Brady. Her eyes were red-rimmed and swollen. But neither tiredness nor grief could disguise the passionate anger there.

In a voice that was hoarse with shouting, she asked a simple question.

'Where do we start?'

BESTSELLING FICTION FROM ARROW

All these books are available from your bookshop or news-agent or you can order them direct. Just tick the titles you want and complete the form below.

☐	ALBATROSS	Evelyn Anthony	£1.75
☐	1985	Anthony Burgess	£1.75
☐	THE BILLION DOLLAR KILLING	Paul Erdman	£1.75
☐	THE YEAR OF THE FRENCH	Thomas Flanagan	£2.50
☐	EMMA SPARROW	Marie Joseph	£1.75
☐	COCKPIT	Jerzy Kosinski	£1.60
☐	CITY OF THE DEAD	Herbert Lieberman	£1.75
☐	STRUMPET CITY	James Plunkett	£2.50
☐	TO GLORY WE STEER	Alexander Kent	£1.95
☐	TORPEDO RUN	Douglas Reeman	£1.95
☐	THE BEST MAN TO DIE	Ruth Rendell	£1.75
☐	SCENT OF FEAR	Margaret Yorke	£1.25
☐	2001: A SPACE ODYSSEY	Arthur C. Clarke	£1.75
☐	THE RUNNING YEARS	Claire Rayner	£2.75
☐	HESTER DARK	Emma Blair	£1.95

Postage ____

Total ____

ARROW BOOKS, BOOKSERVICE BY POST, PO BOX 29, DOUGLAS, ISLE OF MAN, BRITISH ISLES

Please enclose a cheque or postal order made out to Arrow Books Limited for the amount due including 15p per book for postage and packing for orders both within the UK and overseas.

Please print clearly

NAME ....

ADDRESS ....

....

Whilst every effort is made to keep prices down and to keep popular books in print, Arrow Books cannot guarantee that prices will be the same as those advertised here or that the books will be available.